THE LAST CHANCE FOR LOGAN COUNTY

LAST CHANCE FOR LOGAN COUNTY

LAMAR GILES

Illustrated by **DERICK BROOKS**

VERSIFY
Houghton Mifflin Harcourt
Boston   New York

Versify® is an imprint of Houghton Mifflin Harcourt Publishing Company. Versify
is a registered trademark of Houghton Mifflin Harcourt Publishing Company.

hmhbooks.com

The text was set in Adobe Caslon Pro.
Hand-lettering by Maeve Norton
Cover design by Whitney Leader-Picone
Interior design by Whitney Leader-Picone

The Library of Congress Cataloging-in-Publication Data is on file.
ISBN: 978-0-358-42336-2

Manufactured in the United States of America
1 2021
4500833043

For Blueberry

1

A Storm of Frogs

"*YOU ONLY KNOW SOME of the things, Don Glö!*" said the panther-fur-clad warrior-rebel Nanette through the tinny speakers of Grandma's TV.

Sheed, sprawled on his belly with his chin cupped in both hands, gasped. His cousin, Otto, rocked to the edge of the couch, as if tugged by an invisible string. Their grandma shook her head and sucked her teeth. "You better tell 'im, girlfriend."

It was Sunday night in Logan County, and they were tuned in to their favorite fantasy show, *The Monarch's Gambit*. A half-eaten bowl of popcorn rested in easy reach of them all, though everyone had lost interest in snacking as the tension of this critical episode ramped up.

The show's hero, Don Glö, had just been confronted by the Queen of the Warrior Clan. She claimed to have game-changing information about who should be the rightful ruler of the mythical Falcon Steads—giant bird creatures capable of shooting pure light from their beaks. For whoever controlled those beasts controlled the world! But, just as Nanette unfurled the scroll containing the ancient prophecy, there was a scream among her troops. The wealthy and villainous Manticle family picked that very moment to launch an attack.

"No!" Sheed said, rising to his knees in startled surprise. "Not now."

Thunder grumbled in the distance.

Otto hopped from his seat and trotted to the window. A dark, heavy cloud moved their way, and within it lightning flashed like bad thoughts in an evil brain. In his head, Otto echoed Sheed's sentiment. *No, not now.* For different reasons.

"All right," Grandma said, pushing up from her recliner. "Lightning and thunder. Y'all know what that means."

Otto did the unthinkable and paused *The Monarch's Gambit*—something usually forbidden during their sacred hour on Sunday nights. He sensed much worse coming and hoped for a miracle that would allow them to resume the episode, though the chances were slim. Sheed was on his feet, clearly panicked, his palms thrust forward in a gesture of peaceful reasoning.

"Grandma," he said—*begged!* "Please, there's only, like, twenty-five minutes left. That storm is way, way out."

Lightning washed the room in a white flare, followed immediately by thunder close enough to rattle the popcorn bowl. Sheed's shoulders sagged.

Grandma was not without sympathy. "I want to see what happens, too. But you know we don't watch no TV while the Lord's doing His work."

Otto wanted to debate this house rule. Had, in fact, challenged it in the past. Grandma was raised to believe that during storms, using electrical devices could "draw the lightning to you." Otto, studious in his science classes, knew that wasn't exactly how lightning worked. Yes, it could follow the path of least resistance through an electrical pole or antenna. Yes, a strike could fry devices with a direct connection to whatever the lightning struck. In Logan County, though, where most of the electrical wiring (including the wiring to their house) was underground, the chance of such a thing actually happening was very low. So low, they should definitely risk getting struck to see the end of *The Monarch's Gambit.*

"Gran—"

"Octavius Alston, I'm not doing this with you tonight. I know all those things about lightning you're fixing your mouth to tell me, but there's something you just can't argue. This is Logan County. Anything can happen. Now, do as I say—cut that TV off and unplug it from the wall."

Sheed, who could not dispute the county's tendency

to produce improbable events, still looked like he might hyperventilate. "If we *unplug* everything, the DVR won't record the last half of the episode."

"Creek it later. Like y'all always talking about."

"*Stream* it," Otto corrected, so distraught he didn't even think twice about the dangers of correcting Grandma. They *could* stream the episode later, but it usually took a day or so to appear on their streaming service. Which meant even if this were a short storm, they'd have to wait until tomorrow to know what happened. *After* everybody else at school who wasn't forced to unplug everything saw. It'd be impossible to avoid spoilers.

Grandma dismissed Otto's correction with a wave. "Creek. Stream. The only thing I'm concerned with is UN. PLUG. Don't make me say it again."

With that, Otto and Sheed approached the TV like two pirates walking a plank. Sheed slid the TV from the wall; Otto grabbed the thick cable of the power strip and yanked it from the outlet. Nanette and Don Glö winked away.

A heavy sheet of rain crashed against the ground, roof, and windows. It became a fast patter with an occasional heavy *THUMP* that made Otto, Sheed, and Grandma crane their necks.

"Is that hail, Grandma?" Otto asked.

"Can't rightly say. The weatherman ain't call for no rain to begin with, so this surprise storm could be a surprise *hail*storm, I suppose."

4

THUMP-THUMP.

Those thumps were the heaviest yet, and the house shook. A picture frame leapt off the wall, shattering the glass on the wood floor.

"Oh," Grandma said, "I don't like that at all. Let's get into the closet."

THUMP-THUMP-THUMP-TH-TH-TH-THUMP.

Otto and Sheed shared a look, both thinking their own version of the same thought. This wasn't a normal storm.

Grandma left the den and yanked open the closet door beneath the staircase. "Boys, right now."

They weren't going to argue, but before he could get his butt in gear, Sheed heard a new sound, a *SMACK* instead of a *THUMP*, and traced it to the nearest window. When he saw what caused it . . .

"Grandma, you should probably see this."

She stomped to him. "This better be important because I am not in the habit of repeating myself, Rasheed Alst—"

Grandma stiffened next to Sheed, so of course Otto needed to know what the fuss was about. He strolled to them, while the whole time the odd hail-like noises outside went rapid-fire.

THUMP-THUMP-THUMP-SMACK-SMACK-THUMP.

Next to his grandma and his cousin, Otto saw why.

The heavy somethings *THUMP*ing down among the torrential raindrops weren't hail.

They were frogs.

Fat green frogs.

The *SMACK* sound was them leaping from wherever they landed and affixing themselves to the windowpanes by tiny suckers on their webbed feet. As Otto stared at a plump, pulsing frog the size of a baseball on the center of the pane, two more leapt from the rainy night to join it. *SMACK-SMACK.*

"Ewww," Sheed said, more grossed out than alarmed. The frogs smeared snotlike slime on a window he and Otto would definitely have to clean when things were dry again.

More frogs thumped on the roof. And more still

smacked onto other windows. Grandma said, "I've seen a lot in my years here, but this is new."

Otto said, "Not exactly. There have been tales of small-scale frog storms in Logan before. I have a note about it in one of my Legendary Logs, and—"

"Not now, Octavius."

Otto said, "All I mean is it could be worse."

Grandma and Sheed scoffed. That was something you never, ever said in Logan County. He should have known better.

"Come on," Otto said. "They're frogs. Regular, every-day—"

The fat baseball frog raised up on its legs like it was doing a push-up, angled its face toward the glass. It grinned, sort of, showing a mouthful of glistening, needle-sharp teeth. It began working those teeth against the glass, scoring it with a sound like metal grinding. Its comrades did the same. They seemed really hungry, and probably not for windows.

Grandma and Sheed stared at Otto, narrow-eyed.

Logan County. Where anything can happen. Where things can always get worse.

True to form.

Otto could only shrug. "My bad."

2

Strangers at the Door

"OTTO," GRANDMA ORDERED, "Get the phone. Call the county sheriff."

Otto ran for the handset, picked it up. "Line's . . ." He almost said *dead,* but reconsidered. "Not working."

"What about your cell phone?" Sheed asked.

Grandma was already digging in her purse, shaking her head and mumbling what was probably bad words. "I left it in the car."

Sheed said, "That's why it would be super helpful if me and Otto had our own phones."

"Not now. Closet, closet, closet!" Grandma yelled, though hiding in their usual storm spot probably wasn't going to help them. Frogs were attempting to chew through the windows, as well as the doors. The boys could hear those little teeth working the wood like tiny buzz saws.

Grandma rummaged through the closet, grabbing at

various junk they'd usually push aside so they could squeeze in until a storm was over. She handed items to the boys like a medieval armorer handing swords and shields to anxious knights.

"For you." She gave Otto an old catcher's mask and a baseball bat.

"And you." She handed Sheed a snow shovel and a rust-speckled miner's helmet with a tiny spotlight mounted on the front.

"Why do you have a miner's helmet, Grandma?" Sheed asked.

"Oh, that don't belong to me."

Sheed peeked under the brim. Faded Sharpie marker spelled the name *SOLO*.

"Here." Sheed pushed the helmet toward Otto, wanting nothing to do with it, and took the catcher's mask. "It'll mess up my 'fro."

Grandma wedged a set of pink boxer's headgear on top of her Sunday wig and armed herself with the biggest umbrella they had.

The front door was visible from where they stood. At the base sawdust spilled on the floor as a rapidly working mouth created the first breach. Not large enough to let a frog through. Yet.

"What do you want us to do, Grandma?" Otto said.

"If they get in, we knock 'em aside." She snatched her car keys from her purse, tapped the Unlock button on her key chain; her car horn honked faintly outside. "If we get an opening, we make a run for the car. Rasheed, you go for the front seat. Octavius, you're going into the back."

Otto was appalled. "Why's he get the front seat?"

"Because them hungry frogs ain't gonna give y'all time to argue over who gets the front seat. So what I said is what I said."

Sheed flashed his widest, gloating grin.

A second hole opened at the base of the door. Glass broke in the TV room. Did a window just give?

Staccato thumping across the hardwood floor and a couple of bloated green amphibians hopping around the corner made it clear that yes, a window did give and now Tooth Frogs were in the house, closing in on Grandma and the boys with their slick, sharp chompers exposed.

Otto and Sheed shouted, "Maneuver #107!" The slap shot.

The boys went to work, Sheed with his shovel and Otto with his bat, using the equipment like hockey sticks.

They smacked the frogs airborne. The amphibians cartwheeled end over end, emitting a sort of screaming *RIBBIT* sound as they flew behind the couch and into a potted plant, respectively. The maneuver worked perfectly, but more frogs kept spilling inside. Six of them. Nine. A dozen.

Those holes at the bottom of the door had widened, allowing more Tooth Frogs through.

Grandma opened her umbrella and shoved it forward

like a plow. The Tooth Frogs made their displeasure known with angry croaking before setting their teeth to the nylon shield, shredding it.

However, a narrow path had been cleared. Grandma yelled, "Boys, come on!"

She reached for the doorknob but stopped a mere millimeter short when the biggest *THUMP* yet knocked at the center of the door! The force of it sent vibrations through the floor. It was nearly strong enough to splinter the wood. Otto had a single, terrifying thought. *How big is* that *frog?*

Three more powerful *THUMP*s hammered the door, followed by a gruff voice. "Open up!"

"These frogs can talk?" Sheed said.

Not that they hadn't encountered talking animals before, but none had tried to break into their home and eat them.

The boys flanked Grandma, and she spread her arms wide across their chests, nudging them along as she backpedaled. There wasn't far for them to go. The chorus of *RIB-BIT*s behind them grew louder, and the numbers of Tooth Frogs multiplied. They were trapped.

The weakened door couldn't stand up to the next big blow from whatever was on the other side. The lock shattered, and the door swung in, trapping some frogs between it and the wall. New frogs hopped through the open door presenting those needle teeth, but Grandma and the boys focused on the shadowy figure in the doorway.

It stood like a man, a hood raised over its head. Lightning flashed around it, and then it became two. Or, rather, a second hooded being—smaller, also draped in shadow—made itself known. The larger one stepped inside, juicy raindrops sluicing off what the boys now recognized as a black raincoat. The second being followed. Their faces remained hidden in gloom.

Grandma said, "It's in your best interest to leave our home. As quick as you came."

"It's our home, too." The larger figure slipped a hand beneath his hood and flipped it back, revealing a familiar, and unexpected, face.

The smaller figure flipped her hood back, releasing a springy mane of hair. "Hey, Ma."

Grandma, stunned, dropped her shredded umbrella. The boys were shocked, too. Though not so much they couldn't manage a single word each.

Otto said, "Mom?"

Sheed said, "Dad?"

A Tooth Frog said, *RIBBIT*, but no one cared much about that anymore.

3

Family Reunion, Incorporated

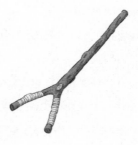

THEY SHOULD'VE BEEN MORE WORRIED about the frogs, of course. The amphibians were still there. Hungry. With the teeth. Yet, the concentrated *RIBBIT*s were like a distant roar from a county over. Otto and Sheed struggled to understand the What-How-Why of their parents being before them, together, after months away.

A comforting sort of instinct made Otto reach for his notepad, to jot observations (matching raincoats . . . they were prepared for a storm no one knew was coming, and they're together despite not having been on great speaking terms over the last couple of years) and deductions (something forced them here . . . but what?). Before he could satisfy his habit of intricate record keeping, Otto's mom knelt, her arms wide, and said, "Come here, sweetie."

He became a toddler again, lumbering toward her happily, wanting to nuzzle his face in the crook of her neck and smell the lavender soap on her skin. Otto hugged her so tight . . . before becoming alarmed and pushing her to arm's length so they were eye to eye. "Where's Dad? Is he okay?"

Mom nodded reassuringly. "On company business down in Georgia. He's fine. Promise."

While relief washed over Otto, Sheed felt something else entirely.

"Hey, champ!" His dad said, stuffing his hands in his coat pocket and focusing on his shoes.

"Hey," Sheed responded, dragging his gaze anywhere else. Good thing, too—given the onslaught he was quickly reminded of. "Frogs! Frogs!"

They were a full army now, closing in.

One leapt and bit down on the hem of Otto's Mom's raincoat.

"Lovely," she said. She flicked the frog away—it took a hunk of coat with it—then twisted toward the open door. With a hand cupped around her mouth, she shouted, "Gentlemen, could use an assist here!"

A sound the boys mistook for more thunder drew near. It was footfalls. Black boots connected to yellow hazard suits worn by masked men dragging two huge vacuum hoses into the house. The thick tubes were the same bright yellow as their protective gear. The hoses were wide and heavy enough that it took eight men—four on each hose—to handle the cumbersome weight. It reminded Otto of firemen hanging on to a powerful water hose. The men at

14

the front of each hose spoke from behind mirrored face-plates, their voices nasally through the circular respirators. "Power on!"

Switches were flipped, and the *Whirrrrrrr* of a forceful motor drowned the *RIBBIT*s as the hoses sucked up startled Tooth Frogs as easily as Grandma's vacuum snatching crumbs off the floor.

There was clear panic in the eyes of the frogs. Most leapt toward the TV room in retreat, while the unlucky ones clung to the walls, windows, drapes, vases, and anything else they could affix their sticky webbed forefeet to while their muscular hind legs flapped like flags in the new suction. The vacuums were too strong, and frog after frog dislodged from whatever they'd stuck to with a *glup-glup* sound.

As strange and bitey as the frogs were, Otto felt for them. "Mom, are they being hurt?"

Mom shook her head vigorously. "Oh no, sweetie. GOO, Inc., is a humane company."

Uncle Solo rolled his eyes. To which Otto's mom sucked her teeth. As strange as it was to think, Otto found some comfort in that bit of normalcy — siblings Cinda and Solo Alston had been at each other's throats for as long as Otto could remember.

Cinda grabbed Otto's hand, tugging him outside. "I'll show you."

Solo said. "Come on, son. We gotta see this."

Sheed watched Otto and Aunt Cinda step into the cool night hand-in-hand and felt a twinge of jealousy. Not that he necessarily wanted to hold his dad's hand, but . . . maybe . . . it would've been nice if that was an option?

Solo kept his hands stuffed deep in his coat pockets, his focus on the exit. As usual.

Sheed quickstepped ahead of him, following Otto. Grandma trailed, shouting. "Wait, wait, wait! Is it safe out there?"

Solo made a sort of wobbly motion with his hand. "Eh. As safe as Logan County ever is, Ma. Storm's over, if that's what you mean."

They all went together to see what was what, and it was something to behold.

There were more men in full-body hazmat suits and more hoses, all snaking into trucks with big potbelly containers attached to them. The containers had motors mounted on top for the vacuum and something like portholes on the sides that let you see in. Or let the captured frogs see out. Several of them pressed their bulging eyes to the glass, their mouths moving with silent *RIBBIT*s. Stenciled in big block letters on the side of each truck: GOO, INC.

The company trucks had Grandma's house surrounded.

Even the frogs that tried to escape through broken windows were being sucked up. Otto told his mom, "This seems excessive."

"*Thorough*," Cinda insisted. "It's the GOO way."

"Spoken like a true corporate automaton," Solo said.

And here we go, Otto and Sheed thought at the same time.

An automaton was like a robot, Sheed knew. An insult. Aunt Cinda wasn't going to let that go.

She said, "Spoken like a true *slacker*. Must be nice to bounce around the globe as you see fit, with no real responsibilities."

"Oh! So acquiring the Scroll of Infinite Joys and Sorrows from a vampire warlord wasn't responsible? Plucking the Ruby Eye from a gorgon, no big deal?"

Otto's brain exploded. "Vampire warlord? A gorgon?"

Uncle Solo's adventures were always so, so incredible! Light-years beyond the stuff him and Sheed got mixed up in here in Logan. Otto pawed his pad from his pants pocket and scribbled notes.

Cinda shot back, "Please, tell me, dear brother. How much of that helped pay Ma's mortgage and medical bills?"

They took a few more verbal swipes at each other over the same things they always took swipes at each other about, and no one seemed to notice the vacuums had been deactivated (all Tooth Frogs collected, presumably), so all the suited and booted men could listen to the escalating argument, too. The gap between Cinda and Solo Alston had decreased as they screamed into each other's faces, and it was only the single, louder voice every Alston feared that stopped it from going too far.

"ENOUGH!" Grandma shouted, forcing everyone in earshot to flinch. She looked smallish wedged between her two grown-up children, her pink boxer's gear crooked on her head, but also somehow like a giant that could crush them all.

With everyone cowed into silence, Grandma said, "Now. More pressing matters. What are you two doing here?" She swept an arm toward all the trucks. "And what is all this?"

Cinda and Solo spoke at once, the words unintelligible. They stopped and exchanged dirty looks.

Grandma muttered, "Good Lord," then motioned to Cinda. "You first."

Sheed noticed the satisfied expression on Aunt Cinda's face, the complete opposite of his dad's obvious irritation.

Otto thought his mom could've been a little nicer to Uncle Solo, given the hard times he'd had over the years, but knew better than to say anything about it. Trying to stop those two from fighting was like trying to soak up ocean waves with a sponge. A never-ending, unwinnable task.

Cinda reached inside her raincoat and produced a thin tablet. It was the latest model GooPad, not even on the market yet. Otto salivated. She tapped, swiped, hemmed, hawed, then flipped the tablet around for them all to see a complex multicolored map of Earth. "One of the new GOO, Inc., communications satellites picked up an unusual energy source while orbiting over Hong Kong a couple of weeks ago. It was weak but just weird enough to capture our attention. We started seeing it daily, always around midday. Our science department determined it was weak in Hong Kong because it was *originating from somewhere else*. Like if you threw a rock into a pond and created ripples. Whatever the original energy source was, it sent ripples all around the world. So, after recalibrating our older satellites to follow those ripples back to the source, we—"

Solo interrupted. "Need a quadrillion dollars in satellites and fancy tablets to tell you what any observant dabbler in the arcane could piece together with a few seances? You've really gotten soft in your old age, sis."

"I'm eleven months younger than you!"

"That 'energy signature' is actually a powerful spectral beacon. Every Ouija board in Argentina just about went airborne when it first popped last month. The ghosts I've encountered recently can't shut up about it."

"Ghosts!" Otto wrote that down.

Cinda shook her head and tapped her tablet. "There is an aspect of spectral energy, but it's also broadcasting across the mortal coil."

"Guess your fancy equipment is good for something."

"More than you are."

"Children!" Grandma regained control and waved to her son. "Continue."

Solo said, "Bottom line, Ma . . . I went looking for the cause of this strange energy spike, and it led here. To Logan County."

"Specifically, this patch of land." Cinda showed a zoomed-in satellite image of Grandma's house, and the trucks surrounding it, and all of them standing just off the porch.

Otto said, "Whoa! That's a real-time image?"

Cinda directed her pointed response at Solo. "Just a little something a quadrillion dollars of tech is capable of."

Solo stomped toward the house, climbing the porch steps while freeing something from inside his coat. It was forked, Y-shaped, crooked as a tree branch . . . Maybe it used to be a tree branch.

Sheed said, "Is that a divining rod?"

"Sure is! Carved by some senior practitioners of the strange arts. It'll help me pinpoint the exact source of this odd new energy emanating from the land." Solo stepped inside the house holding the forked ends of his rod like the reins of a horse.

Cinda came on the run, tapping her tablet screen. "No need for such rudimentary methods, bro. GOO, Inc., has an app that'll handle it from here."

"An *app*? Please."

Sheed, Otto, and Grandma followed the eternally competitive siblings as they trekked all over the house in a race to prove which one of their methods was better. Giving Otto time to note some of the night's observations . . .

OTTO'S LEGENDARY LOG, VOLUME 32
Entry #7

This is one of the weirder nights we've had in Logan County in a long time, and that's saying something. Not because of the Tooth Frogs, either. My mom, Sheed's dad . . . here at the same time?

Deduction: As happy as I am to see Mom and Uncle Solo, I got a feeling big trouble came with them.

Solo's rod yanked him upstairs, while Cinda followed the spinning dial on her screen into the kitchen. Then they switched, and backtracked, and bumped each other's shoulders aggressively in passing.

"Trace energy appears to be all over the place," Cinda said.

"For once we agree," Solo responded.

Otto and Sheed and Grandma watched their expressions change from determined, to frustrated, to perplexed.

They angled their devices toward the family, taking slow steps. Sheed wondered if maybe they'd given up, until they met each other's eyes in a way that didn't seem like two cats wanting to fight over a loose sardine.

"This can't be right," Cinda said.

"No. No. No," Solo said.

The tablet and the divining rod angled in the same direction.

At Sheed.

4

Those Dang Side Effects

"UHHHHHHH," SHEED SAID, STARING at the wavering tip of his dad's divining rod and wincing at the frantic beeping of Aunt Cinda's tablet.

Otto wedged himself between the adults and his cousin, grinning awkwardly. "Gotta be a mistake," he said, having a strong sense that it wasn't a mistake, as well as an equally strong sense of *why* it wasn't a mistake.

The Fixityall that Sheed took in Warped World to save his and Otto's life; the miracle medicine they were warned could have stunning side effects if Sheed returned to this reality.

Cinda tilted her head, scrutinizing her son. "What are you hiding, Otto?"

"Hiding?"

"Yes. I know that you are, because when you're hiding something, you repeat words that I say to you."

"Repeat?"

Cinda swept Otto aside with her forearm, aiming her tablet at Sheed. "Are *you* going to tell me what's going on?"

"No," Solo said, bumping Cinda aside with his hip. "He doesn't like all your fancy-schmancy tech screeching at him." To Sheed, he said, "You wanna tell *me* what's going on. Don't you, son?"

Grandma snatched off her headgear and pointed toward the kitchen. "Everyone to the table right now! Someone is going to tell *me* something. Believe that."

All obeyed. All sat. Except Grandma. She ruled. "Someone explain everything to me before I count to three. Because y'all don't want to know what happens when I count to three. One, two—"

Sheed broke. "Fine. I was going to die, then me and Otto went through a mirror into another dimension with medicine that fixed me, but they told us there'd be side effects, and I guess that's what's happening."

Otto shook his head and let it thunk on the table. Cinda and Solo blinked slowly, their mouths twisting. Grandma cocked her head, spoke gently. "One more time. But slower."

\#

They told it all, with Otto taking a break in the middle to grab the Legendary Log he'd kept when they'd gone through the last mirror on the left, so he didn't mess up any details. Missus Nedraw. The Judge. Nevan the Night-mare. The Spinsters (or the dance crew formerly known as

ArachnoBRObia). And, of course, the Fixityall, with its ominous warning of potential side effects.

When they finished, Cinda pressed back in her chair, arms crossed, staring at Otto. "You let him take some strange medicine from another reality?"

"*Let* is a strong word," Otto said.

Sheed jumped in, trying to take his equal share of the blame. "I had to, Aunt Cinda. Otto was in trouble, and I wasn't strong enough to help. I took the medicine to save him."

Solo pressed his palms flat against the tabletop, as if that were the only way to keep them from shaking. He still couldn't look at Sheed, and when he spoke, no one was sure if he was addressing anyone in particular or simply verbalizing an unthinkable horror. "You could've *died*?"

Otto knew some of what Uncle Solo felt. He'd spent weeks living with the possibility of a mysterious sickness that might one day take Sheed from them all. When the threat was a real thing, Otto could barely eat, or sleep, or think of anything but life without his beloved cousin. Since they'd used Missus Nedraw's Black Mirror to confirm that Sheed would live to a ripe old age, Otto had had the best days and nights of his life. Infinite optimism and sound slumber. Things he knew Uncle Solo had gone without for a long time. Because of the person he *couldn't* save. Sheed's mom.

Cinda twisted in her chair. "Ma, you didn't know anything about this?"

"I most certainly did not," Grandma said.

"That is very troubling. The arrangement we've all made is based on —"

Heavy knocks sounded on what was left of the front door, interrupting his mom. Yet it didn't stop Otto from thinking, *What arrangement?*

Cinda sprang from her seat. "Oh, shoot."

She left the room in a hurry; Otto ran after her. Sheed followed him. Solo followed Sheed. Grandma brought up the rear. "Not more frogs, is it?"

"No, Ma," Cinda said, strain in her voice. "Probably the head of my support crew. I'll send them away until we figure out exactly what's going on with Rasheed."

But when she left the house, her expression shifted to a deep frown. No one was on the porch.

"Hello?" Cinda said.

Otto sensed the change. It was quiet. Too quiet for a platoon of hazard-suited support crewmen to be surrounding the house with a fleet of giant vacuum trucks. The only sounds were the *pitter-patter-drip* of leftover rain falling from the roof. This was wrong.

Sheed felt it, too. An emptiness that shouldn't be.

Then Cinda leapt, startled. "Oh. Ma'ams. What are you doing here?"

Otto scooted outside, as did Sheed, Solo, and Grandma, flanking Cinda.

26

On a patch of grass beyond Grandma's porch was a new vehicle. A long and fancy limousine with its nose pointed directly at the family. It was glossy black, with dark, impenetrable windows, though three passengers' heads poked through the open sunroof like fingers through a moth hole in a shirt.

The women were wedged closely together, shoulder to shoulder. Alone in an empty yard.

No trucks. No toads. No vacuums. No men.

"Where did everyone go?" Sheed asked.

"Mom," Otto said, "who are they?"

"We are the . . ." said the one on the far left, with a voice that reminded the boys of puppets on television, overly deep and projecting.

"Joint heads of . . ." said the second lady in the middle, in a similar tone.

"The GOO Corporation," finished the third lady on the right.

Which wasn't creepy at all. Noooo. Not one bit.

They were pale ladies, their luminescent skin made all the more extreme by their black suit coats. They each had the same short, dark bob haircut. Their jewelry was teardrop earrings and golden necklaces that dangled crystalline stones, and very smart-looking wire-rimmed glasses. These women could've been mistaken for triplets, but something about them seemed unlike siblings to Otto. Twins, triplets, quadruplets were all still different people . . . These three seemed like *the same woman*. The only differentiating features were their turtleneck sweaters: red, blue, and green.

Cinda stammered, "I'd like to introduce you to my family. My mother, son, brother, and nephew. Family, this is Missus—"

"Nyar . . ."

"Latho . . ."

"Tep."

Missus Nyar. Missus Latho. Missus Tep. Otto jotted that down.

Cinda shuffled off the porch for a closer conversation

with her . . . bosses? She said, "I was planning to send you a status report in the morning."

"Yes, but we thought . . ."

"It was prudent to . . ."

"Examine the grounds ourselves."

"Oh, certainly," Cinda said. "I can brief you on everything that's happened so far. But I assure you I've got things under control."

"Have you identified . . ."

"The source of . . ."

"The energy pulses?"

Cinda stiffened.

The Heads of GOO, Inc., leaned forward, spoke in unison. "Well?"

"No," Cinda lied. The entire Alston family knew the most likely source of the energy pulses *sensed around the globe* was Sheed. All of them maintained unmoving faces so as not to give the secret away. Regardless of any bickering, messy arrangements, or lingering crankiness, the family had each other's backs.

Cinda's bosses scrutinized them.

"Well, we trust . . ."

"That you will . . ."

"Continue your search."

Cinda's shoulders relaxed; she seemed surprised by their response. She asked, "What are you three going to be doing while I'm searching?"

They sprouted synchronized smiles. "Shopping."

They descended into their limo, and the sunroof closed with a mechanical whine. The limousine reversed course, then turned onto the county road toward the town of Fry.

Missus Nyar, Missus Latho, and Missus Tep were gone. To shop. Whatever that meant.

The family shuffled into the house, exhausted and shaken. Cinda and Solo directed the boys to bed. Otto and Sheed knew the adults weren't going to sleep, and they'd be talking about Sheed, but they were worn out from all the excitement, so bedtime was fine for once. Plus, they had their own brief discussion before lights-out.

Sheed said, "You think those ladies your mom works for are evil?"

Otto thought on it only a second. "Definitely. Good night."

He clicked off the bedside lamp like normal, snuggled beneath his blanket, and turned to the wall while Sheed did the same on his side of the room. But instead of falling asleep almost instantly like he'd been doing in the weeks since they left Warped World, Otto stared at nothing, too anxious to doze.

Sure, almost getting eaten by carnivorous frogs that rained from the sky might upset one's sleep patterns. There was more to it, though.

It shouldn't have been this way, but Mom and Uncle

Solo showing up out of nowhere felt as ominous as the night's first storm cloud.

Stop it, Otto told himself. *There's a lot to think about, but you'll think better after some sleep.*

He turned over to click off the bedside lamp. Except, he already did that.

So why was the room so bright?

Otto sat up in the yellowish sheen that pulsed dull, then bright, then dull again with the rhythm of a heartbeat. He swung his feet to the floor and stared at Sheed snoring softly and glowing eerily.

Yellow light rimmed Sheed, bright enough so Otto could see through his cousin's blanket like he had X-ray vision.

Otto reached across the gap between beds to wake Sheed, but stopped himself, his fingers hovering a few inches shy of Sheed's shoulder. He was in a sound sleep. Peaceful. Otto didn't want to rob him of that, because he had a strong feeling it might be a while before Sheed would get to relax again.

Since he was taking on the burden of a mild freak-out for both of them, he might as well note his observations. He grabbed the Legendary Log off the nightstand.

ENTRY #8

Sheed's glowing.

Mom said the energy pulses they tracked back here first got their attention in Hong Kong, midday. I don't know exactly what time it is there, but I'd be willing to bet it's midday right now.

This happens every night!? He's like a freaking light bulb!

Maybe the strongest light bulb ever if the energy he's putting off reaches around the whole world.

In this case, does strong mean dangerous?

Deduction: I don't have any way to tell what this glow is, or what it does. But I know who might. I think it's time for a trip to the doctor. Hopefully, we won't catch fleas.

5

Are Were-Men a Thing? Hmmmm.

OTTO HAD LEARNED HIS LESSON about keeping secrets from Sheed, so as soon as his cousin was awake, Otto told him what he observed. He told Sheed about the glow.

Sheed listened. Feeling a little annoyed, he said, "You should've woken me up."

Otto said, "You're right. If for no other reason, to have this talk before you got morning breath."

Sheed became *really* annoyed. After he brushed his teeth, they continued the conversation. "So the Fixityall side effects . . . It's making me glow like a firefly when I sleep?" Sheed sprang up, twitchy, and started tugging on his school clothes. "Let's talk more on the way to town."

"Okay." Otto was already dressed and ready (he loved being ready for school), but was puzzled by Sheed's eagerness. Until Sheed started knotting together their sheets.

"Oh," Otto said. "Maneuver #87?" Maneuver #87 was a bedsheet escape.

"You know they're not going to let me out of the house after last night."

He had a point. An easier maneuver might work if it was just Grandma. Mom and Uncle Solo were a whole other problem.

Sheed anchored the improvised rope to his bed frame, hoisted their window open, then threw his looped home-made rope outside, looking nervous about the whole thing.

Otto triple-checked that he had his science homework in its proper blue folder for an easy reach-and-drop on Mr. Rickard's desk while thinking of ways to reassure Sheed that he'd be fine scaling the side of their house on some suspiciously unstable-looking sheets.

Cinching his backpack straps tight on his shoulders, Otto said, "It's this or be under their microscope all day."

"You mean under their tablet and divining rod."

Their parents would want to know more about whatever energy was coming off Sheed. Would be bickering about it the entire time. Otto couldn't really blame them. He wanted to know more, too, particularly since Mom's obviously evil bosses were involved.

So if they didn't want their parents getting all adult-worried about a problem they could probably handle on their own, it was the bedsheets for Sheed.

Otto said, "Count to fifty, then go, I should have them all good and distracted by then."

Sheed tugged at the anchor end of the sheets to make sure it'd hold. He did not look convinced.

Otto thought his distraction could be one of those two-birds-with-one-stone things. He'd gather the adults in the kitchen, then announce he wanted to practice a science presentation. This would be very exciting to them, he figured. While he was explaining photosynthesis through a series of interpretive dance moves, Sheed would be shimmying down the side of the house. Only a loud snore interrupted Otto's plan.

Grandma's bedroom door was cracked; she was a clearly visible lump beneath her blanket. Her chest rose and fell in time with the grizzly bear snore that made her lips flap. He kept going down the hall and found his mother in the guest room, curled into a bundle like a pill bug. Frowning at the increasing possibility that he would not get to rehearse what he called his "Dance of the Green," he trudged down the steps and found Uncle Solo knocked out on the couch, his socked feet twitching while he dreamed.

Did they stay up all night? All for Sheed? And what was discussed?

"I knew I should've bugged the kitchen," he mumbled, taking the time to note the task on his lengthy to-do list.

Otto made it to the side of the house where Sheed was

halfway down the wall, clutching the sheet-rope in a death grip.

"Where are they?" Sheed said.

"Sleeping. You're good."

"Oh, that's what's up. I was really worried for a minute —argghhh!" The rope gave, and Sheed fell into the bushes.

"You all right?" Otto said, his mind on photosynthesis and wondering if Sheed might have stunted the growth of the bush that caught him.

Sheed rolled out onto the grass, spitting leaves. He stood, smoothing wrinkles from his clothes and scanning every direction to make sure no one witnessed his momentary lapse in coolness. "I'm fine. I'm fine."

They grabbed their bikes and headed to town, figuring whenever everybody woke up, they wouldn't go as far as to come pull Sheed out of school. The boys could surely count on one day of peace at least. That wasn't too much to ask.

They were earlier than usual, having built time into their schedule for extra maneuvers to help Sheed escape, if needed. Biking past the WELCOME TO FRY, VIRGINIA sign, they expected the normal morning bustle of the town and were not disappointed. Workers milled into City Hall clutching coffee cups and chattering into cell phones. Mr. Archie dragged his power washer onto the Main Street sidewalk to clean some grime off the concrete. Miss Remica cracked her door and let the savory scents of her fresh pastries unfurl into the atmosphere. The Rorrim Mirror

Emporium sat dark, feeling cold and empty ever since Missus Nedraw left, and that gave both boys an unexpected sense of sadness each time they passed.

Turning off the east-west run of Main Street, they headed south, coasting alongside a school bus full of their classmates on its way to D. Franklin Middle School. The big rolling block of yellow cheese puffed dark exhaust clouds while the notoriously jolly bus driver, Ms. Carmichael, waved from behind her wide steering wheel. All the sights, sounds, and smells were familiar. Particularly the oily-batter scent of the Monte FISHto's fast food chain, the marquee beneath the giant fish sign reading NOW SERVING BREAKFAST.

Sheed, who'd skipped his usual bowl of Frosty Loops to facilitate his escape, had a rumbly tummy, and for a brief moment wondered what a place like Monte FISHto's might serve for breakfast, but quickly dismissed the thought. He wasn't *that* hungry.

They took a turn and passed the park, which was mostly empty this early except for a Fry familiarity in Mr. Feltspur and his infamous kites.

Mr. Feltspur went to Grandma's church and didn't have anyone at home because his kids were grown and his wife passed away years ago. In his spare time, when church ladies weren't putting on their good wigs and their perfume, and bringing him food he didn't ask for, he built kites. Not regular kites, either. Some were shaped like animals—he had a creepy octopus one with tentacles that moved like it was swimming through the air. Sheed hated that one. Then he had one that was shaped like the Stealth Bomber. It was huge, and he had to use a special rig to manage the string. That was Otto's favorite. There were a bunch in between. Some big, some small. Today's was shaped like a UFO, and Mr. Feltspur guided it in a tight circle over his head.

He waved, the boys waved back, and Otto thought about Grandma seeming super frustrated whenever Mr. Feltspur's name came up. "Dang fool gonna mess around and get snatched away if a wind gust catches one of them kites wrong, I swear."

All in all, the ride was what they were used to. Even the taste in the air, a sweet tickle of dewy grass on the tip of the tongue. It should've been comforting.

"Doesn't look like Tooth Frogs rained down on anyone else, does it?" Sheed said.

Otto tried to make light of it. "Maybe the storm hit a different part of town. Or it could be like those times when you can stand on one side of the street that's dry while the other side is getting drenched by rain."

Sheed didn't respond. That in itself was a response. He was concerned about the frog storm over Grandma's, as was Otto, though he was determined not to let it show. Which led to another oddity, Otto's pleasure at seeing Wiki and Leen Ellison on the next block with their bikes discarded on the ground while they . . .

Stared at a stop sign?

Otto squeezed his handbrake and hopped off his bike at the curb. Sheed did the same, his focus where it always was.

"Hey, Leen." Sheed began picking his Afro unnecessarily. Preening, Grandma would've called it.

"Hey, Sheed." Leen flashed her biggest, brightest grin, like someone was about to take her picture.

Otto and Wiki groaned, rolled their eyes, then grimaced when they noticed they were doing the same thing, then grimaced again at their matching grimaces.

Leen said, "Can you guys believe what happened at the end of *The Monarch's Gambit* last night? Who would've thought that Don and Nanette are—"

Sheed shrieked and held his hands palms out as if fending off an attack. Otto plugged his fingers into his ears. They spoke in unison, "No spoilers!"

Leen's mouth snapped shut.

Wiki chuckled. "Good luck getting through today."

Otto unplugged his ears. "What are you doing?"

Wiki slowly circled the sign she'd been scrutinizing. "Wouldn't you like to know?"

"Oh, stop it!" Leen said. "They might be able to help."

"But I don't want their help, sis."

Leen blurted, "There's possibly a were-man on the loose in Logan County."

"No there's not," Wiki said, producing a pair of tweezers

from her pants pocket, using them to pluck something off the signpost.

Sheed's goofy grin fell off his face. "What's a were-man?"

Leen spoke rapidly. "Wiki said there's no such thing as were*wolves*, and I said, what about were-men? Like, maybe a man can't turn into a wolf, but what if a wolf can turn into a man? She agreed that might be possible."

"I didn't agree," said Wiki, squinting at a long brown hair pinched in those tweezers.

Otto said, "You two are definitely not telling us the whole story here."

Wiki snaked a hand into a pouch on her satchel and fished out a plastic evidence baggie (it actually said EVIDENCE in big block letters) and a vial. She opened the vial, dropped the hair inside, then resealed it. Otto snatched his pad from his pocket.

ENTRY #11

We need baggies. And vials.

Wiki said, "There have been reports about a strange man sneaking around downtown businesses the last couple of nights after everything's closed. Mr. Lopsided caught him hanging around the loading docks behind Lopsided Furniture. Said the guy was extremely hairy, and jumpy

—he knocked Mr. Lopsided down, then apologized profusely before bounding away."

Sheed said, "Bounding?"

"That what's Mr. Lopsided said. Bounding. Moving in long hops instead of running. Leen checked traffic cams, and the camera from that ATM." Wiki cocked her head toward Fry Savings and Loan across the street. "The video doesn't give a clear look at him, but he's short, he was indeed bounding, and he snagged his coat rushing past this sign. We decided to check it out and, boom, clue." Wiki wiggled the vial.

Leen said, "Were-man hair! Boom."

"No, sis."

Otto reached for the vial, wanting a closer look, but Wiki dropped it in her bag before he could even touch it.

"Hey!" Otto said.

Wiki smirked. "We can talk about it some more after me and Leen solve this mystery and get another Key to the City. How many would that be for us?"

Leen joined in the gentle gloating then. "Four, I believe."

"Four!" Wiki leaned toward Otto, waggling her finger between him and Sheed. "And how many do you two have? One . . . each?"

Otto didn't go for any of his usual comebacks. Instead he sprinted to his bike, hopped on, and pedaled away, yelling over his shoulder as he went, "Well, too bad you can't beat me to school."

A bike race was a challenge none of them could resist any more than a dog could ignore a juicy bone. There was a mad scramble from Sheed, Leen, and Wiki to grab theirs and catch up. Otto's head start was insurmountable. As was his irritation.

Still, he'd take a win however he could get it.

6

Things You Catch at Night

THE LEGENDARY ALSTON BOYS and the Epic Ellison Girls were still racing when they rocketed through the halls of D. Franklin Middle School on the way to Mr. Rickard's science class. It was a heat so close that they wedged themselves into the doorway. Otto gritted his teeth and wriggled his way across the imaginary finish line, then spun around to face his competitors, proclaiming, "First!"

He mistook the troubled expressions on the faces of Sheed, Wiki, and Leen as the look of sore losers. Which, of course, made him want to boast more, until he realized how odd it was that their classmates were all seated and unusually quiet before the morning bell had sounded.

The only noises in the typically chatty room were the squeaks of Mr. Rickard's marker on the dry-erase board and the sporadic thumping of the large cardboard box bouncing on his desk.

Otto immediately thought, *Boxes shouldn't do that.*

Mr. Rickard, a tall, wide man with two tufts of white hair sprouting from the sides of his otherwise bald head, didn't look away from his scribblings when he said, "Sit down."

On any other day, the man would've been smiling, jovial, ready to champion the fun of science to his students. Today, though . . .

"Sit. *Down.*"

Sheed, Wiki, and Leen moved cautiously to their desks, watching Mr. Rickard the way they'd watch a tiger who'd escaped the zoo. Otto—who felt he had a good rapport with teachers, Mr. Rickard being no exception—thought a well-timed inquiry was in order. Because the box was still bouncing.

"What's that?" Otto said, pointing.

Mr. Rickard remained focused on his whiteboard, though he did answer the question. "Something I caught at my house last night."

From inside the box came a moan.

Otto decided it was best to take his seat.

He slid into his desk in the back row next to his cousin, glad for the distance between him and Mr. Rickard's mystery box.

The bell rang, officially starting class. Mr. Rickard did not seem to care. He scribbled on.

Sheed leaned into the aisle toward Otto, whispered, "Cuzzo, that seem strange to you?"

"How could it not?"

Wiki occupied the seat in front of Otto's. Leen, the one in front of Sheed's. They twisted around with twinlike synchronicity to talk to the boys.

Wiki said, "We might be in trouble here."

"Yeah," Otto agreed, "because Mr. Rickard doesn't like us talking during class."

"Really, Otto? I don't think that's going to be an issue today. He's not worried about us at all."

Leen dug some cobbled-together goggles from her bag and fitted them over her eyes, the lenses as dark as onyx. A row over, Madison Baptiste snapped her fingers and said, "Girl, you look fierce!"

"Thanks! I love your braids." Leen tapped a button on the side of the goggles, nodded, then, "Yep, definitely in trouble. I can't tell what's in that box, it's sort of blurry on my infrared, but it's warm, and getting warmer."

The box leapt again, and one of the flaps popped open. A hot draft filled the room as if someone had cracked a window on a summer day.

Mr. Rickard scrawled his final words, dotting one last *i* so hard, it seemed like he wanted to jam his marker through the wall. He tossed the marker aside, then faced the class. His body blocked most of what he'd written, though the visible words to the right and left of him were . . . bad. The kinds of words Grandma might make them scrub their eyes for seeing.

"So, kids." Mr. Rickard, bug-eyed, with his pupils looking odd in a way Otto couldn't quite pinpoint, pulled a folded slip of paper from his breast pocket. "Do you know what this is?" A slick bead of drool rolled down his chin.

Nobody said anything.

Mr. Rickard unfolded the paper. "It's a check."

Otto couldn't read the writing on it from the back of the room.

Leen, having adjusted her goggles, whistled. "That's a *big* number." Then, to Wiki, "What's a check?"

"A form of currency exchange, Evangeleen!" Mr. Rickard, who'd never made a movement quicker or more strenuous than lifting his PeteyTech coffee cup to his lips, hopped on his desk with the agility of a jungle cat. Everyone in the front row yipped. Even the mystery box stopped bouncing, like it was shocked.

Leen said, "I still don't know what a check is."

Sheed knew. Grandma used some of the very same bad words on the board when she had to send checks to the electric company, and the water company, and the cable company. Sheed whispered, "Mr. Rickard got paid for something."

Mr. Rickard caught the quiet statement, his hearing

46

sharp. "Paid is an understatement, Rasheed. This money is the money owed someone who answered an ad for a science teacher thirty years ago, *in good faith*. Someone who moved to a town because he was told there was no other candidate better than him. When the school board really meant there was *no other candidate*. Because no sane science teacher wanted to come to the most illogical town in the whole dang world! Do you understand what it's like to try to teach reason in a place where, sometimes, people disappear through mysterious portals? Do you?"

Otto raised his hand but didn't wait to be called on. "No, sir. Because none of us are teachers."

"THAT'S NOT THE POINT!"

Otto put his hand down.

"Whatever weird thing you stop, counter, attempt to disprove in this county, another stranger thing comes along, weirder than before."

Now, that was something everyone in the room understood.

Mr. Rickard hopped off the desk, still waving his check. "This money is a gift from the real estate gods. They've saved me from being stuck in this weirdo town until the day I die. Woo-hoo."

Real estate meant property, houses and land. Maybe someone bought Mr. Rickard's house?

With that, it hit Otto . . . He knew why Mr. Rickard's

pupils looked strange. He could identify the shape they'd taken, as if they'd become more pronounced in that very second.

His pupils looked like dollar signs.

The teacher no longer blocked the things he'd written on the board with his body. The bad words weren't the main point of his scribblings. The overly large letters in the middle of the mad, curse-word laden ramblings were. Two words: *I QUIT.*

"Well, kiddos, I'd like to say it's been a pleasure. But, no." With the flourish of a veteran showman, Mr. Rickard took a bow like he expected applause, then motioned to his final message for the faculty, staff, and students of D. Franklin Middle School. "Consider this my letter of resignation."

He cackled again, positioned himself like a sprinter waiting for a starter pistol. Then he thrust himself toward the nearest window, and dived through the glass.

Everyone ejected from their desks, rushed the now broken window to see if Mr. Rickard had hurt himself, careful of the scattered shards of glass themselves. He appeared to be fine—in the loosest sense, physically at least—as he jogged away, howling laughter, waving his check like a victory flag.

Otto, Sheed, Wiki, and Leen worked their way to the front of group crowding the window.

Sheed said, "Mr. Rickard don't seem okay, yo."

Wiki patted him on the shoulder. "Great observation."

Otto said, "We should probably get somebody. Like, the principal."

There were low murmurs of agreement; it seemed the best option.

Bryan Donovan said, "Mr. Rickard forgot his box."

Mr. Rickard wasn't the only one who'd forgotten about that box. It hadn't bounced in a while, perhaps that was the reason Bryan felt okay doing what he did. In the split second it took for the boy to reach for the flaps and open them, Otto and Sheed only had time to think, *Noooooooooo!*

Something exploded from the box in spinning, frantic motion. It collided with the ceiling tiles, denting them and raining dust. With it came a mighty howling gale like the gusts of air before a maelstrom, forcing everyone to hunch and shield their eyes from all the classroom debris that had suddenly taken flight.

Papers fluttered. Pencils propelled. A few desks closest to the box flipped end over end. Fortunately, no one had been hurt. Yet.

Still, neither Otto nor Sheed could quite make out the force that was causing all of this.

Or, rather, they didn't want to believe what they saw. Because it made absolutely no sense.

It looked like . . .

A head.

Free-floating. No neck. No body.

Also, not an actual head, because *ewwwww*. It looked more like a *sketch of a head*. You could see the lines that made up its angry eyes. Its chin and hair that whipped about in the furious breeze. Most noticeable were its puffed-out cheeks and a series of additional curled lines that spilled from its puckered lips, like slurping up spaghetti noodles in reverse.

It was crazy. As crazy as it was, Otto, Sheed, Leen, and the rest of the class recognized it was also familiar.

Of course, Wiki, who never forgot anything—especially a face—reminded them all who they were in the company of.

"Hey," she said, "that's the Wind."

7

The Winds of Change

LET'S BACK UP A SEC . . .

Mr. Rickard, back in the days before he went loony, once did a lesson on oceans and continents. In that lesson, he showed the class a series of maps from various points in history, explaining that explorers from centuries ago believed very different things than what science has proved in modern times.

At the edge of some maps, beyond the point where the mapmaker would've put other continents if they'd known about them, was a warning declaring "Here there be Tygers" or "Here there be Dragons" or—Otto's favorite—"Here there be Monsters."

"When other continents were eventually discovered," Mr. Rickard had said, "the maps changed appropriately."

In that instance, Sheed had raised his hand and did not wait to be called on. "They thought it was Tygers with a *y*, but then they're *discovering* stuff. How could they discover land that people already lived on? It sounds like you're giving them too much credit."

Mr. Rickard's face got rosy red. "These men, for their time, were the greatest minds in exploration."

Sheed pointed to the drawing of a poofed-up head in the top corner of a map blowing breezy breath over the land and seas. "They thought Wind was a person, though."

Now Sheed knew he owed the mapmakers an apology over the Wind-as-a-person (or at least a head) thing. He wasn't backing off the you-can't-discover-land-people-already-lived-on thing, though.

The Wind zigzagged around the room, blowing stuff every which way. Aside from the dark lines of its sketchlike features, it was see-through, nearly invisible if you tried to spot it from the wrong angle. Its power was fully on display, like a tiny hurricane set loose in their science room.

Kids dived beneath the chairs. Others saw an opening and darted into the hall, hopefully to get help. Frankie Cartwright tried to hide behind Morty the class skeleton, and the Wind drew down on them, snatching Morty and Frankie up into a macabre airborne dance.

Otto, Sheed, and the Ellisons took cover behind Mr. Rickard's desk. Leen dumped her bag, spilling a pile of gear she'd invented. The soda cans she'd shaped into various devices and circuit boards from old computers were easily identifiable among her wares. What all that stuff did was a question only she could answer. She plucked through her inventions, tossing some aside while mumbling, "We don't want any acid, so no . . . and lasers would probably be as bad as acid, so no . . ."

Sheed said, "Maneuver #62?"

"I don't think we can get everyone evacuated, then seal the room without someone getting hurt," said Otto. "We still gotta get Frankie down."

Frankie drifted around the ceiling, holding Morty by the waist in a rough approximation of aerial ballet. He said, "I'd really appreciate that, guys."

Wiki pointed to the nearest corner where the Wind's prior prison got tossed. "That box—can we get it back inside?"

Otto said, "Maybe. We distract it, you trap it?"

Leen glanced to Wiki, who nodded, then said, "We find your plan agreeable, if not wholly innovative, but whatever. Let's do it."

They fanned out, Otto and Sheed waving their hands to draw the Wind's attention and darting to the opposite side of the room while Wiki and Leen went the other way. The Wind twirled toward the boys, blowing a gust of air that hurled Otto in the opposite direction he'd intended to go in. He landed right back behind Mr. Rickard's desk.

Sheed was still on the move, and the Wind chased, bearing down on him. When he reached the corner, with nowhere else to go, the Wind descended to eye level, and the two began a staring contest. Through the apparition's nearly transparent features, Sheed saw the Ellisons holding the cardboard box between them, tiptoeing through the perpetual draft, attempting to recapture it. The Wind was not concerned with anything but Sheed, its eyes traveling up and down the boy's body as if he was as strange to it as it was to him.

Wiki silently mouthed a countdown. *Three, two . . .*

The girls leapt, and the Wind immediately blew a megagust from its backside, hurling them away.

Wiki cartwheeled, but her landing was cushioned by classmates who saw her coming. Leen was less fortunate, flying toward the dry-erase board and colliding with the wall, giving her head a nasty sounding *THWACK!*

"NO!" Sheed shouted, furious.

For the duration of a single eye-blink, Otto saw his cousin flash yellow, like a light bulb flicked on and off.

The Wind . . . winced.

Its previously angry, gusty expression transformed to something like shame. The megadrafts circulating through the room decreased by half. Enough for Frankie and Morty to drop to the floor. Enough to turn the maelstrom of loose papers into a bunch of lazy leaves swaying to the ground.

The Wind, seemingly downtrodden, jetted through the same window Mr. Rickard broke and disappeared into the skies over Fry. Everything in the wrecked room settled down.

Sheed rushed over to Leen, who was shaking off whatever stars that blow to the head had her seeing. Wiki and Otto joined him.

"You okay, sis?" Wiki said.

Leen grinned. "I'm fine. When I hit my head, I got this really great idea about how to possibly make a black hole."

Otto said, "*Is* that a great idea?"

Their principal—Missus Hader—rushed in, the few classmates who'd escaped the Wind's early barrage on her heels. "Is everyone all right?"

Calming by the second, everyone brushed themselves off and confirmed they were fine.

Sheed pointed at the board. "Mr. Rickard left you a note."

Missus Hader read it and blushed. "Oh dear. Avert your eyes, children. Avert your eyes."

Over the next half hour, the entire school was ushered into the auditorium while the faculty and staff conferred about how to handle the rest of the day. Sure, the incident had been contained to one classroom. But a teacher going insane and releasing an elemental on school grounds would probably make it hard for everyone to concentrate.

After much hand-wringing, Missus Hader came onstage, tapped the microphone to make sure it was working, then reluctantly announced, "Due to unforeseen circumstances, we will be forced to release you early to—"

The rest of her message was drowned by a standing ovation and subsequent chants to elect the Wind class president.

With everyone filing out for buses or bikes, or relocating to the cafeteria if they didn't have a way home yet, the Alstons and the Ellisons hung close together. Sheed and Leen nuzzled shoulder to shoulder, while Otto remained super focused on the contents of his locker to avoid a conversation. Wiki wasn't having it.

She said, "Are we going to talk about it?"

"I don't know what you mean," Otto lied, reaching for the new highlighter he'd put in his locker last week. He'd need it when he reviewed the Legend Log later. Only . . . it wasn't there.

He pawed along the locker shelf, beyond his neatly arranged pens, pencils, and erasers.

"What's wrong?" Wiki peered over his shoulder.

"My highlighter. It was right here."

"Oh please, Otto. Stop trying to change the subject."

"I'm not trying to change the subject!" He wanted the subject changed, but he wasn't *trying*. He really was missing a highlighter. And it wasn't the first time he'd put something in his locker only to come back and find it missing. Weird. Could there possibly be a thief in D. Franklin Middle?

Or *thieves?*

Otto wondered . . .

Wiki spun him around by the shoulders. "The Wind! Sheed scared it off. Didn't you, Sheed?"

Sheed fiddled with his Afro pick. Leen cocked an eyebrow like she'd press the issue, so he gave her that side-of-his-mouth goofy grin Otto caught him practicing in the mirror once. Leen pretty much melted, so she wasn't going to be a problem.

Wiki was not so easily dissuaded. "Like I thought."

"What do you want me to say?" Otto closed his locker, forcing himself to forget his missing school supplies and focus on avoiding Wiki's interrogation. "We don't know why the Wind got startled by Sheed's yelling."

"You know *something,* though."

"Do you see my liar tic?"

Begrudgingly, she said, "No. You're not lying to me *right now.*" She focused on Sheed. "Even though there's something going on with you. Seems like y'all are as clueless as I'd normally expect."

They made their way outside to the bike rack. Sheed said, "You wanna help us figure it out?"

Leen perked, close to a yes. Wiki clamped a hand over her sister's mouth before she committed. "We've got our own thing to deal with first."

"A were-man?" Otto scoffed.

"*Key,*" Wiki said, full-on attitude, "*to the City.* Once we're done with that, maybe we'll grant you some assistance. To the bikes, Leen!"

"Bye, Sheed," Leen said.

"Bye, Leen," Sheed said.

The Epic Ellisons trekked off, but before they disappeared entirely, Leen said, "I don't know how closely related to Mr. Rickard going crazy that Wind creature was, but I saw something else when I zoomed in on that check thingy."

"What?" Otto asked.

Leen said, "GOO, Inc."

Otto and Sheed kept their faces fixed until the Ellisons were gone. Once they were left to their own devices, Sheed said, "Dude, your mom's obviously evil bosses, what, bought Mr. Rickard's house?"

"They said they were going shopping. If they bought Mr. Rickard's house, I think we can assume it's not for a good reason."

"Did his new insanity give it away?"

Otto's face got serious. His hand twitched.

Sheed knew the look. "Go on. I know you want to. I'll just stare at the sky or something while you do."

Otto flipped out the Legendary Log again!

ENTRY #14

We have a Tooth Frog storm last night, Mom, Uncle Solo, and GOO, Inc., show up.

58

There seems to be mysterious energy pulsing off Sheed, strong enough to be felt around the world.

Mr. Rickard goes absolutely nuts in front of the class, waving a check from GOO, Inc.

A mythical elemental nearly sweeps the whole class away, only stopping when Sheed yells at it.

Deduction: This is all so much weirder than usual, and that's saying something!

Sheed whistled, practiced a couple of roundhouse kicks, mumbled something about needing to get a hobby for when Otto had to scribble all of his brains on that stupid pad.

Otto tucked his notes back into his pocket, chewed his bottom lip.

"Well?" Sheed said.

"We can't keep pretending we don't know at least part of what this relates to."

Sheed's shoulders slumped. "My side effects."

When they were in Warped World and got warned something *might* happen, Otto also received instruction on what to do if something *did* happen. "It's time to see Dr. Medina."

Sheed's shoulders slumped further, his knuckles almost dragging the ground. "She's a *veterinarian*, Otto."

"I know, but she's the closest thing we've got to being able to . . . *diagnose* stuff like this." Or so he'd been told.

Sheed huffed. "Fine. But I'm not putting on one of those dog cone collar things. Bet that."

8

The Doctor's Order

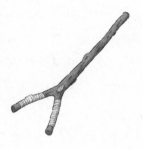

TECHNICALLY, THE INSTRUCTIONS OTTO received after Sheed took the mysterious medicine known as Fixityall were to return to Warped World to see the dog-headed version of Dr. Medina, the version most familiar with the medicine, should anything strange happen with Sheed. That required access to the Rorrim Mirror Emporium, something that hadn't been available since Missus Nedraw left to shut down mirror prisons in other realities. The doors weren't merely locked. They were magically sealed. Otto knew because he'd tried getting in a few times when Sheed had slept late, allowing him to slip away. Just in case.

With the emporium unavailable, it meant a trip to their local vet. Upon entering her office and triggering the door chimes, the receptionist, a parrot sheathed in emerald and orange feathers, greeted them. "Have a seat!" it cawed. "Read a magazine!"

The boys settled into the only two chairs in the tiny waiting area. Otto checked the magazines but couldn't see himself enjoying the latest issue of *Animal Fitness* with everything going on (though the cover sloth looked quite healthy in her headband and designer sweat suit). Sheed couldn't stop squirming, as if his seat cushion was really a bed of nails.

"It's going to be fine," Otto said, knowing no such thing.

"You're not the one about to be examined by someone who neuters cats."

Neither of them knew what *neuter* actually meant, but it didn't sound fun.

Dr. Medina pushed through the swinging doors separating the waiting area from her examination room, peeling off a pair of rubber gloves and looking just a little bit annoyed. "Figured it was you two. Thanks for saving me the trouble of coming to find you."

Otto said, "Coming to find . . ."

"*Us?*" Sheed finished.

"Yes. Something strange is going on, and I'm fairly sure you two are involved. Nothing new there, right? Everybody knows the sorts of things the Legendary Alston Boys get up to, I'd just hoped you'd continue to leave me out of it." Her eyes narrowed behind the lenses of her glasses. "Follow me."

She disappeared behind those swinging doors. The boys scooted along after her.

The corridor and a larger exam room filled with cages were mostly identical to the versions they'd visited in Warped World . . . though much quieter. Eerily so. When they joined Dr. Medina at the exam table, they felt every animal eye in the place on them—from lizard to bear cub—though no animal uttered a sound.

"You hear that?" Dr. Medina said. "Nothing. Not a peep. You know when that happens?"

Sheed said, "Whenever we're nearby?"

"WHENEVER YOU'RE NEARBY!"

Sheed had said "we." Otto sensed this was all about Sheed's side effects. But Otto was willing to take whatever heat came over what they'd done in Warped World. All the way to the end.

Dr. Medina pulled a giant machete from beside her examination table. Otto wondered if the end was going to be right now.

Sheed backpedaled toward the door. "What's that for?"

The doctor removed a coconut from a sack near the machete sheath, then chopped it in half, spilling the milk without concern. "Lunchtime for all the new mimes here."

Aside from the coconut, she produced carrots, and star-fruit, and bananas, and more. The silent animals got twitchy with excitement when Dr. Medina divided the fruits and veggies on her desk into manageable chunks for her patients.

She filled tiny bowls for a cat in a cast, and a dog with an eyepatch, and a gerbil with a rash. All took their food quietly; the only noise came from their tiny teeth chewing. Sheed cringed the whole time. "I really wish you'd all start barking, growling, or something."

Just like that, the animals resumed their usual noises.

Dr. Medina cocked her head, a mannerism very similar to her Warped World counterpart with the canine features. "Hop on the exam table right now!"

The command was so sharp and precise, Sheed felt like he had no choice but to obey. He hopped onto the table while Dr. Medina grabbed instruments from a cabinet. She faced him with a stethoscope, the ear/throat thingy with the built-in light, and an air of grim determination.

"Open wide and say ahhhhhhh!"

#

It went on for two hours. Dr. Medina looked down Sheed's throat, peeked in his ears, made him do jumping jacks, checked him for ticks (Otto mentioned that might not be necessary since Sheed wasn't a dog; Dr. Medina reminded him it was never a bad idea to check for ticks). After every test she frowned, consulted some manual or other, then began some new form of examination that had both boys antsy from the never-ending nature of it all.

After, like, the fiftieth test, Dr. Medina disappeared into a back closet for . . . something. While she rummaged,

Otto said, "I'm sorry. This is a big waste of time. Maybe we should go home and see Mom and Uncle Solo."

"No! It's weird enough that they're back. That's a separate problem, and"—Sheed hopped off the exam table, shuffled foot to foot—"I just don't want to deal with them right now."

Not *them*. Sheed really meant he didn't want to deal with *him*—as in his father. Otto didn't press the matter. Family was nothing if not complicated.

Dr. Medina returned to the exam room with a new device that looked . . . intimidating. In one hand she gripped a long wand. A curling cable stretched from the wand to a boxy device in her other hand.

"Is that . . ." Otto squinted. "A Geiger counter?"

"Sort of," said the doctor.

"You think I'm radioactive?" There was a quake in Sheed's voice.

"This doesn't measure radiation." She flipped a switched on the device with the wand angled in Sheed's direction, and a loud clicking immediately filled the room, setting the animals and the humans on edge.

"I'm radioactive!" Sheed yelled.

Dr. Medina nudged the wand closer to Sheed; the clicking became a nearly unbearable shriek that cut off suddenly as the meter box in the doc's hand glowed red, then belched a plume of gray ozone-scented smoke.

She gawked. "That device is one of my own invention, one I found necessary after my first-year practicing in Logan County. I'd take in animals with the normal range of animal ailments and injuries, but when I crated them and left them to sleep at night, my cameras would catch a soft glow. My first thought was radioactive exposure, but that proved to not be the case. No gamma rays, no beta or anything else that made sense. When I got used to how things were around here, I theorized there was another form of energy present—unique to this county. I built a device to track it accurately, and the energy coming off you, young man"—she pointed a shaky finger at Sheed—"fried its circuits like a potato in hot grease."

Otto asked the question Sheed was likely too afraid to. "What are we talking about here, Dr. Medina? What kind of energy is coming off my cousin?"

"I call it U-rays . . . as in *uncanny*. You might know the energy by its more common name. *Weird.*"

Sheed plugged his fingers into his 'fro, as if he might tear his hair out. "You're saying I'm radiating *weirdness*."

"More powerfully than anything I've ever seen, and that's saying something for Logan County."

"But what does that mean?"

"Well—" Dr. Medina began, but was interrupted by the chittering door chimes, followed by an extended, "BaaaaaAAAAaaaa!"

Dr. Medina perked. "Oh, that's my lunch! Come on back, MJ!"

A goat—blue-gray fur, with a white tuft around the mouth—trotted into the exam room with a grease-stained bag dangling from its teeth. The familiar logo for Monte FISHto's covered the front side of the paper sack. Dr. Medina took it, unfolding the creased bag top with barely contained anticipation.

Sheed, confused, said, "I think we should definitely take a lunch break now."

Dr. Medina missed the sarcasm, or just didn't care. "Totally. I'm starved."

"Doctor," Otto said, in what Grandma called his persuasive sweet-boy tone, "Maybe this isn't the time—"

"Hey!" said the doctor, her face etched with confusion . . . though not from anything the boys had said or done. "What's going on, MJ? This order's wrong."

The goat said, "Baaaa-aaa-aaaa."

Dr. Medina flopped in her seat, massaging her temples.

Sheed felt ridiculous asking her this, all things considered, but said, "Are *you* okay?"

"It's just puzzling, is all. The other day Michael Jordan came in with this bag from Monte FISHto's, and—"

Sheed made a timeout T with his hands. "The basketball player?"

"No. Don't be ridiculous. The goat's name is Michael Jordan. It's right there on his name tag."

Sure enough, there it was. A tiny bronze tag dangling from the goat's collar identifying it as Michael Jordan. Otto made an O with his mouth, like he might say something, but nothing he might say seemed like quite enough in the moment.

Dr. Medina went on. "So, MJ brings me this bag out of the blue. I didn't ask for it, didn't even know I wanted it. When I open it, though, it's my favorite thing on FISHto's menu . . . Double Cra-Burger with Cheese and large Filet Fries. Yum! The next day, it's the same thing. Then, on the third day, I thought it'd be fine if MJ brought me another Cra-Burger but I wouldn't *mind* a Flounder Patty. Guess what happened . . ."

Otto said, "Michael Jordan the Goat showed up with a Flounder Patty."

"Right! A couple of days later, I thought some Carp Nuggets might be good, and . . ."

Sheed said, "The goat named Michael Jordan came with some Carp Nuggets."

"Every day for two weeks, if I thought about a particular item from FISHto's, MJ brought it. Once or twice I tried to think of a different restaurant, like Mia's Italian on Route 9, but I guess MJ has a certain range, and FISHto's is the only thing in it, so he'd bring me something I was thinking about from there. Then, today, I thought an Octo-Salad with French Dressing would be great, but that's not what was in the bag. This"—she held up a sandwich wrapped in a waxy paper—"is a Double Cra-Burger with Cheese, something I haven't thought about in weeks. Isn't that weird?"

"No!" Sheed snapped.

"It's a little weird," Otto said, but Sheed was in a tantrum now.

"According to you," Sheed said, "*I'm* weird—or I'm radiating weird—whatever! And you won't tell us what it means because your lunch order, that you didn't really order, is wrong?"

"You're going to want to watch your tone with me, young man."

The goat named Michael Jordan said, "Baaa-Aaa!"

Out front, in the waiting room, the door chimes sounded. A new visitor.

Dr. Medina slam-dunked her unwanted Cra-Burger back into the greasy bag. "Who on earth could that be?" She left Otto and Sheed to ponder what they'd learned.

"*U-rays?*" Sheed said. "That's ridiculous."

"Is it, though?"

"She made that up, Otto."

"Maybe the name, but don't you think the concept sounds solid? At least a little?" He flipped out the Legendary Log.

"Don't!" Sheed warned. "Consult. Your notes."

Otto consulted his notes. "We knew that something was coming. We've been waiting for it ever since Warped World. And, it *has* been weirder around here."

"Because some frogs fell from the sky? Because we met the Wind from old maps? We've seen way weirder stuff."

"True," Otto said, scribbling. "We always had to *find* weird stuff, though. Go on a quest. Lately, it's been finding us."

"You mean finding me."

Otto shrugged.

Sheed said, "So what? Is this 'I'm going to die' all over again? Do we ever get to relax, cuzzo?"

"I don't think it's that. We know we're both going to live a long time, the Black Mirror showed us. Give me a sec to get this all down."

"Please, take your time. I'll just be over here hanging out with Michael Jordan."

The goat chuffed, scratched at the floor with one hoof.

ENTRY #19

U-rays! I like it. Don't tell Sheed.

But, really, what's this all mean? Uncanny Radiation. Considering the morning we've had, it's funny because I wish (a not-crazy) Mr. Rickard was here. In a lesson not so long ago, he talked about how not all radiation is dangerous. Some of it is very bad, like the kind that comes from nuclear bombs. Some of it needs to be used very carefully. It's why you put on that heavy lead blanket when the dentist X-rays your teeth. Sometimes everyday items have radiation, like bananas.

(None of us believed that, but Mr. Rickard passed around an article that said it was true.)

Deduction: I don't think Sheed's V-rays are nuclear dangerous. I don't know if they're banana harmless, either. I have a strong gut feeling if there's any danger in the V-rays, it may not be for Sheed.

Sheed picked his 'fro and stared at Otto with very little amusement. "I'm ready to go."

"Fine. Chill. I think we have enough for now. Dr. Medina!"

She'd been gone awhile, but when Otto called her name, heavy footsteps clacked toward them. At the same time, the animals—docile just a second ago—began to rattle their cages. Their hisses and barks and meows and honks became an unsettling concert. Sheed leapt off the examination table, wedging his pick in his hair. Otto pocketed his Legendary Log and stepped into a fighting stance. The animals knew something was wrong, as did Otto and Sheed.

"Maneuver #11," Sheed said, all business. *Be ready so you don't have to get ready!*

Dr. Medina pushed through the swinging double doors with force, sporting a clown grin. Her lips peeled back showing every tooth in her head, almost like *she* was an animal.

Also, her pupils were dollar signs.

She stood in the doorway, blocking the path to the front. This moment stretched, and Otto was certain Dr. Medina didn't blink the entire time.

Sheed said, "Doc? It may not be my business, but what's up with the shovel?"

Oh, right. The shovel. She gripped the wooden handle like she wanted to crush it. The sharp spade head hovered an inch above the ground. Perfectly still. Waiting to be used.

Dr. Medina, her voice way more calm than when she'd gotten a double Cra-Burger instead of an Octo-Salad, said, "I have work to do."

Otto said, "What kind of work would that be? Seems like your stethoscope would be more useful here?"

She was in motion before he finished the question, rushing them in a jerking shamble. Sheed planted a hand on the examination table and cartwheeled over, making sure to keep something between him and the doctor. Otto tucked his shoulder and rolled to the corner where a fire extinguisher was mounted to the wall. He was ready to grab it and spray the room in a concealing fog if need be.

(There was no maneuver for that, but he'd discuss adding it to the list with Sheed later.)

Michael Jordan the Goat shuffled around, aiming his horns at the woman to whom he'd faithfully brought lunch

73

every day for two weeks, and something in that change was heartbreaking.

Dr. Medina ignored them all, went for the cages.

She was fast. The shovel raised over her shoulder in a way shovels aren't typically used. For a nightmare moment, Otto thought the doctor had lost every bit of her compassion and training and decency, and was about to harm the very animals she'd taken an oath to heal. In the horrible seconds between the shovel rising and falling, Sheed thought he'd reacted too slowly and had been too concerned with his own safety to do what needed to be done and protect the helpless creatures.

The shovel connected with a clang, and the clasp on an iguana's cage fell away. The creature hissed, butted the door open, then leapt from the enclosure and slinked away, never to be seen by Otto and Sheed again.

Dr. Medina took another swing; another clasp fell. That time a cat with a bandaged paw leapt to freedom.

"Doctor," Otto said, "what are you doing?"

"They'll need to find new accommodations." She broke another clasp, freeing what might've been a red panda. "This is no longer a place that can house them."

"You're a veterinarian!" Sheed said.

"I'm not that either." Her wide grin stretched wider. "What I am *is rich!*"

Otto then saw what poked from the breast pocket of her

lab coat. A green slip of paper just like the one Mr. Rickard had waved before leaping through their classroom window.

A check. From GOO, Inc.

The boys knew, without a doubt, they had way bigger problems than U-rays now.

9

The Spindly Sparrows

SHORT OF TACKLING THE DOCTOR, something Sheed had considered, was there really anything they could do to stop her from—what? Breaking the cages that she owned? Setting animals free now that she was rich with GOO, Inc., money and wasn't going to be a veterinarian anymore? She wasn't doing anything technically *wrong*, but at the same time, it felt *all wrong*. All . . . *weird!*

"Come on." Otto shoved through the doors to the reception area, wary that whoever had dropped off that check might still be there.

The tiny room was deserted.

Sheed was on his heels. "We calling someone?"

"I guess—maybe the sheriff?" They'd never actually seen the town sheriff. He or she or they had never showed up when stuff was going wrong before. First time for everything, though.

Otto stopped short of grabbing the telephone. A figure across the street drew his eye. "Sheed."

Yeah, Sheed saw it too. In the alley between the Slawson's Law Firm and Bernice's Bonnet Boutique, a short figure stood. Whoever they were, they were dressed in a trench coat. One hand—the right—was shoved in their pocket; the other reached into the shadows beneath the brim of their fedora to stroke their hairy chin, the only part of their face visible from this distance.

A were-man? Sheed thought.

He jammed a hand into Otto's backpack and freed up the pair of tiny, collapsible binoculars. He unfolded them, brought the lenses to his eyes, turning the focus knobs to sharpen the blurry nothing he was currently looking at. A pair of angry eyes filled Sheed's entire view. It was not the stranger across the street.

Sheed lowered the binoculars. "Dad?"

On the other side of the window, arms crossed and scowl fixed, was Solo Alston.

Beside him, Otto's mom, Aunt Cinda.

Despite what was certainly going to be an unpleasant reunion, Otto leaned sideways for any chance at a better view of the strange figure. Too late. Of course, they were gone.

That was the least of their problems.

Cinda burst into the reception area, followed by her brother. She snapped her fingers at Otto. "Home. Now."

"Wait," Sheed said.

Solo said, "I don't think there was anything unclear in your aunt's order, boy."

Cinda gawked, as if surprised by the backup, then gave her brother a curt, respectful nod. "Let's go, boys."

Otto risked parental wrath to blurt, "Something is wrong with Dr. Medina."

"Wrong how?" said Cinda.

"She's swinging a shovel and letting the animals loose."

A pair of opossums shot from the examination area, hissing their displeasure and aiming their red eyes toward the exit. Solo, courteous, let them out. After they were gone, he mumbled, "Hope they don't have rabies."

Cinda said, "She in the back?"

The boys nodded.

"Solo, like old times."

Solo shrugged out of his leather jacket, then held it before him like a fisherman holds a net. "Cover me."

Cinda told the boys, "Don't. You. Move."

Solo pushed through the doors. Cinda crouched behind him. The boys listened intently, expecting a scuffle, but seconds passed with . . . nothing.

Cinda said, "Clear."

Solo said, "Clear."

Cinda said, "You remember the Spindly Sparrows?"

"I do. I'll give you a boost."

Otto and Sheed flashed confused looks at one another before disobeying Cinda's orders and sneaking to the back, because who wasn't going to investigate Spindly Sparrows?

Peeking around the corner, they found Solo half kneeling. His hands were linked, while Cinda planted one heel in his palms and stretched so she could lift a ceiling tile and look into the narrow crawlspace with a flashlight that must've come from her purse. After moments of scanning the dark, she shook he head at Solo, then performed a backwards somersault, landing in a nimble crouch.

"Figured that was a long shot." She straightened, brushed ceiling dust from her shoulder. "The Spindly Sparrows were a long time ago."

"True," said Solo. "Still nice to rule out those infectious birds."

"For now." Cinda peered around. Otto and Sheed ducked.

Solo said, "We already saw you. You gotta watch your shadows, fellas. Dead giveaways."

The boys glanced down, saw their elongated shadows stretching away from the sunlight beaming through the front windows. Rookie mistake.

They came out of "hiding," performing their own visual search of the room. No Dr. Medina.

Solo shrugged back into his jacket while motioning toward a door at the back. Looked like she took the emergency exit, along with whatever animals had been present. Even Michael Jordan the Goat was gone.

"What happened here?" Solo examined the broken clasp on a dog's cage.

"Better yet," said Cinda, "why'd you sneak out this morning without waking anyone?"

"School day." Otto beamed, hoping to disarm her with his charm.

Cinda activated her Mom stare. "So you didn't think we'd want to talk to Sheed about last night?"

"Y'all ain't say nothing," said Sheed.

Solo said, "Don't go getting smart with your aunt."

Sheed pouted.

Otto, scrambling for some way to keep the conversation from going where he'd knew it'd go—with them on the way home, getting yelled at the whole time—said, "How'd you know where we were?"

"Well," Cinda planted a hand on her hip, "when we figured you'd snuck to school, then we called the school and discovered you'd been released because of 'an incident,' we got worried. Your grandma put the word out to her church ladies, and they know everything, so your location got to us fairly quickly."

Solo said, "*After* we learned Miss Eloise been making goggly eyes at Mr. Winston the truck driver."

Cinda glared.

"What? I'm supposed to ignore all that juicy gossip?"

"Anyhow," Cinda said, "now we got you, and we're going home to talk."

"What about Dr. Medina?" Sheed said, low. Grumbly.

"What about her? Best I can tell, she let the animals go and ran away with them. She's grown, and that's her business, not ours."

Otto's insides clenched. Yes, this was Dr. Medina's place. If she wanted to let the animals go and run off herself, yes, technically it was her business. But, if she was doing it because something wrong was happening inside her, if somehow she'd been . . . what was the right word? . . . *manipulated* . . . wasn't it the business of those around her, people who could help her, to do something about it?

Wasn't it wrong to turn away, like they didn't know she was in some kind of trouble?

Otto said a thing he knew deep down wasn't going to go over well. It was a thing Sheed had wanted to say. Though he knew it was best coming from Otto, because it was going to be his mom that flipped. Oh, boy.

Otto said, "Dr. Medina started acting strange after she got a check from GOO, Inc. Same as our teacher. That was the 'incident' at school. Your company is giving people in town money and, maybe, driving them insane. So this kind of is our business, Mom. Or, at least, *yours*."

Cinda made some jerky head motions; her lips twitched, all expressions of confusion.

Solo, a triumphant grin on his face, waggled a finger in Cinda's direction. "You work for villains! I knew it!"

10

Adult Maneuvers Are Complicated

THE RIDE HOME WAS . . . AWKWARD.

Otto sat in the passenger seat of Mom's 'rental.' Which meant it wasn't her car, and even though it was a huge SUV that could hold, like, a hundred people and had a bunch of cool knobs and levers, it smelled a little like a wet dog.

Sheed sat in the middle row of seats behind Otto, and Uncle Solo sat all the way in the back row because Cinda told him to sit back there—made it harder for him to gripe at her. Sheed kept picking his 'fro, which meant he was nervous. Uncle Solo was dang near giddy, though every time he tried to yell toward the front, Mom clicked a switch on her steering wheel to make the music louder. By the time the tires crunched the gravel in Grandma's driveway, Otto's eardrums were achy.

Cinda was out of the SUV first, but the rest weren't too

far behind. Solo said, "We're not going to talk about your villain bosses?"

"I'm going to speak to my son first. In private. Maybe you should do the same?"

"I don't know. Given the gravity of the situation . . ."

Cinda tossed her rental key at Solo. Hard.

He caught it one-handed, his mood shifting at the prospect of driving the big fancy vehicle. "The situation has changed. Looks like we're going for ice cream, Sheed. Come on!"

Sheed flashed Otto a look, and Otto returned it. *We'll talk later.*

Gloomy, Sheed joined his father in the car, and the tires spit rocks as Solo gunned the engine and rocketed back toward town.

Mom's hand fell lightly on Otto's shoulder. "Come on. We have a lot to discuss."

She led him inside, where they found a note from Grandma saying she'd gone to the market. The way Mom's head bounced when she read it gave Otto the sense that she was happy it was just them for now. He sat at the dinner table without being told. This was definitely an at-the-table discussion, the kind their family reserved for the most serious topics.

Mom rooted around in her big purse for her GooPad. She arranged the fancy case so that the tablet could stand on its own, like a tiny TV screen, then tapped some commands. She said, "If you want to take notes, it's okay."

Otto placed his log on the table, pencil ready, though for the first time in a long time, it didn't bring him comfort. He knew the feeling of "about to hear something he didn't want to."

Mom sat beside him, close, so their faces were displayed back to them by the tablet camera. A ringing sound, like a telephone, came from the device. Then, a momentary pause while the ringing ceased and their faces became a tiny window in the corner of the display. The larger portion was occupied by a round, jolly face Otto was overjoyed to see. "Dad!"

"Hey, buddy! Wait. A. Minute!" Dad leaned closer to his camera, making his face even bigger and rounder on Otto's side. He squinted. Scratched his temple like a detective examining a precarious clue. "Are you growing a beard?"

Otto laughed. His eyes prickled with the delight of seeing his father and hearing his corny Dad jokes. A bit of the joy faded when he noticed the tiny name in the corner of Dad's display: DeMarcusBaker@GOO.com

Reminding him his dad worked for the villains, too.

"D," Mom said, squinting, "you're not in your office."

Dad shook his head. "No, I'm on-site at the new GOO shopping complex. Crunching some numbers and adjusting the estimated time of completion. Seems the crew got a real

burst of energy and is moving ahead of schedule, which will make the bosses *real* happy! What's up?"

"You up for that family chat?"

"Yeah, yeah. This is a good time. You doing okay, son?"

Otto was hesitant to answer. Mom said "that" family chat. Whatever was coming, they'd talked about already. They'd *talked about talking to him about it.*

Mom answered for Otto. "He's under the impression that GOO, Inc., is evil and we work for the bad guys, hon."

"Yikes!" Dad said, clearly surprised. This part hadn't been in whatever they'd rehearsed before. Good!

"I know," said Mom.

"*Evil* is such a strong word. *Bad guys*—pfffttt! Sort of an oversimplification."

"That's what I'm trying to explain to him. Thank you."

"A lot of people get that impression about GOO, Inc. I've been working with the marketing guys on this whole new rebranding campaign. It's called 'What's Evil, *Really?*'"

Mom made a dismissive motion with her hand. "Not now, D."

Otto's stomach was a knot. He spoke low. "It sounds like, maybe, you kind of know the company you work for does bad stuff—like make people go insane by giving them money, or something."

Dad said, "That's what I mean by oversimplification. You say *insane*, but maybe they'd say *excited*."

"*Elated*," Mom offered.

Otto wondered if his parents were the first ones GOO, Inc., drove crazy.

He said, "Why do you work for a company that has marketing meetings about their evil image? Can't you work for someone else?"

Dad said, "That's not as easy as you think, buddy."

"Why not?" The pencil in Otto's hand shook slightly. He wanted so bad to log something that made sense.

Dad's eyes cut left, directly toward Mom. "Cinda, maybe you should take over. This all concerns *your* mother, after all."

Panic punched Otto in the chest. This was *that conversation* — the one they'd prepared for. "Is something wrong with Grandma?"

Mom rubbed his shoulder, trying to be comforting. It wasn't working. "Nothing's wrong with Ma. Nothing new, anyway."

"Is this like how you and Dad are trying to make *bad* and *evil* mean different things? Is something really wrong, and you're trying to trick me?"

His parents flinched. Otto couldn't dismiss the genuine hurt pulsing off his mother.

Dad said, "No one's trying to trick you, son. What we're saying is there's a problem that's always existed. We've tried our best to keep it from you and Rasheed. But it's time that you got a clearer view of the whole picture."

Mom said, "Staying here in Logan County, you, your cousin, and your grandma — together — it may not be an option for much longer."

#

Sheed stared out the passenger window, and Dad tapped his fingers on the steering wheel. A nervous rhythm that sounded like nothing and everything at once.

"Car sure rides smooth, don't it?" Dad said.

"Yeah. Smooth."

Strained moments passed.

"Wanna listen to some music?" Dad clicked the power

button before Sheed decided if he wanted to hear music or not, which was a totally Dad thing to do, so whatever.

A love song was on, an old one. Sheed knew it because it was one from the old records Grandma played on Saturdays when him, her, and Otto had to straighten up the house. Sometimes if it was the kind of song where a man and woman sang together, Grandma would take a part, while Sheed and Otto sang the other—didn't matter which part they took, why should it? The song was still good, even if their screechy, off-key voices weren't.

"*Ooooh-oooh-OOOOOH!*" Dad sang along, or tried to —horrible singing voices ran in the Alston family. "You gonna leave me hanging like that? Come on."

Sheed wanted to be grumpy and keep his eyes on the trees they passed, but he actually liked this song a lot, and it's hard to make yourself not groove when the groove is there. He sang, "*Ooooooh!*"

They harmonized roughly, passed the WELCOME TO FRY, VIRGINIA sign. Dad abruptly stopped singing and hit the brakes when he spotted a bit of a traffic jam ahead. "What in the world?"

A Fry traffic jam wasn't like a big city traffic jam. It was maybe six cars backed up at an intersection. What made this one unusual were the honking horns and one guy leaning from his window and waving a fist at someone else. Fry citizens just didn't get riled up like that.

Something else was off. Sure, people were acting crankier than what was the norm. But, also, some of the cars were different.

Some were local. Sheed recognized one of Mr. Green's classic cars with the chrome and the paint that looked like a candy shell. There was potato farmer Mr. Hannamaker's truck. But there was also one of those fancy new PeteyTech cars that ran on sunlight and water, and the most-out-of-place vehicle was a big, big truck like something the army would use in a desert, except it was painted a glossy red that made it a moving mirror. Its driver was the one making the most noise, even though cars were moving and he could've just been patient.

It was strange to see cars and people like this here. Not that out-of-towners didn't come to Fry; farmer's market Saturdays really were busy here. On a Monday, though?

Because of the extra folks, what should've been a ten-minute trip became twenty. Five minutes of that extra time being the guy in the big army truck deciding he needed to turn around in the middle of the street, blocking both lanes while he inched his too-big vehicle back and forth, yelling at everyone else for simply existing.

Sheed, sunk back into cranky mode, didn't notice when Dad passed the parking spaces in front of the Nice Dream Ice Cream shop.

Dad said, "Where is it?"

Sheed twisted in his seat, extra-irritated and thinking if his dad hadn't been gone so long, he wouldn't forget where stuff had always been. He jerked a thumb behind them. "Back there."

Dad circled the block, came back around, and took the first parking space he saw—wow, the street was crowded this afternoon. They'd have to walk.

So they did. Sheed with his hands stuffed in his pockets, staring at his shoes, while Dad hummed the song they'd sung together. After several yards, Dad stopped. Sheed knew they'd reached the shop without looking up because they'd passed the secondhand store (you could always smell the used books), and the Woodshop (you could hear the buzz saws). Those stores were neighbors to Nice Dream Ice Cream. Only there was a different smell now. Strong, earthy.

Dad said, "I thought it was right here, son?"

Sheed looked up and gasped.

The Nice Dream Ice Cream Shop, which had been right here last week—him, Otto, Wiki, and Leen had gotten double scoops together—was gone. Now it was something totally different. The windows had changed, there were different doors, different lighting inside. It was a . . . a . . . *coffee shop?*

Sheed and his dad stood at the doors, confused for different reasons. Then the guy who'd been driving the army-like truck came rushing up the sidewalk, his arm extended as he thumbed a text on his phone. He wedged himself roughly between Sheed and his dad. "Out of the way, dudes. Need my caffeine."

The rude guy barged inside the shop, letting notes of acoustic guitar twang into the air from the open door.

Sheed finally noticed the name of this new place: *Riches Brew*. He didn't like it, but he liked the small print beneath it, the kind you had to strain to see, even less.

It said: *A GOO, Inc., Company.*

11

The People Who Make Hammers

OTTO DIDN'T WRITE MUCH DOWN. Maybe he would later, if he didn't forget anything. Somehow he didn't think he'd ever forget this conversation.

The more his parents spoke, the more they paused and hemmed and hawed over every new and uncomfortable thing they had to say.

Mom said, "We never wanted to leave you in Logan County, sweetie. There are some grownup realities that you may not have understood at the time, and may still seem complicated and unfair. Me and your dad had to leave here to make money. There aren't enough jobs for grownups here."

Otto didn't think it was complicated, though. His parents were just wrong. "Mr. Archie has a job at his hardware store. Mayor Ahmed has a job at City Hall. A lot of adults work here."

"True," Dad said from the tablet. "But Mr. Archie's hardware store isn't profitable. Do you know what that means?"

No. Otto didn't want to admit that, so he said nothing.

Dad said, "Every month he's always a little short, son. He's not selling enough things to be able to pay people he owes. Like the electric company or—or the people who make hammers."

Mom interrupted. "The people who make hammers, D?"

"It's an analogy. You know what I'm saying, son?"

"Hammers can be bad?"

Dad said, "See? He gets it."

Otto didn't get it.

"I'll take it from here," Mom said. "A lot of months of being short on money adds up, and before very long, you owe a lot of companies a lot of money. It makes it hard to keep your business open. It makes it hard to keep your house, because you have to pay someone for that, too."

"Someone's going to take Mr. Archie's house?" Otto felt near panic. He wanted to go help Mr. Archie, who'd always been good to him, Sheed, and Grandma. He'd almost forgotten helping Mr. Archie wasn't the point. Mr. Archie was *the analogy*—which meant his parents were using the hardware store owner as an example for some other, bigger point. What, though?

Mom said, "Mr. Archie's going to be fine, mostly

because his daughter is married to one of the richest men in the world. Anna and Petey Thunkle have been helping him stay afloat, so that arrangement works for them. Not so much for us. Not anymore."

Otto was one of the greatest detectives around these parts. He'd completed legendary feats. It wasn't hard for him to connect the dots. "You've been helping Grandma keep our house."

Mom exhaled the kind of puffy breath that comes with words you never wanted in your mouth. "Me, your dad, and your Uncle Solo made a necessary arrangement a long time ago, shortly after Rasheed's mom, er . . ."

"Died," Otto said for her.

"Yes." She stroked the back of her hand along his cheek. "You have grown, haven't you?"

Dad said, "For most people, it costs money to stay in a house, son. Your grandma is no different. She's also had some health problems."

"Her sugar, and high blood pressure," Otto said so they knew him and Sheed had been keeping an eye on her and making sure she took her medicine. "A shot in the morning, and a pill at night."

Mom's shoulders sank. The very hand she'd stroked his cheek with cupped her mouth to catch a hiccup. A second passed before Otto realized it was actually a sob. When her eyes got watery, she stood and turned away, hugging herself.

Otto didn't know what he'd done wrong, but apologized anyway. "I'm sorry."

Dad leaned into the tablet display like he might push through the screen and into the kitchen. "You didn't do anything wrong, buddy. Not one thing."

Mom cleared her throat, patted her moist eyes, faced him. "We put too much on you boys. We had to. Ma couldn't work to keep paying all the bills at the house, not being sick so much. The best paying jobs we could get meant we'd have to travel for the company, never one place for very long. That was no life for a little boy—you'd never be able to get settled, never keep any friends for long. And, with what Solo was going through after Rasheed's mom passed, him taking care of your cousin didn't seem like a much better idea. We found a compromise. The two of you would stay here in Logan County to keep an eye on Ma, and we'd all send money to help her keep the house."

This was news, Otto supposed. Him and Sheed never knew exactly what made their parents leave them in Logan County, and they honestly didn't think about it hard because they loved it so much here. "Is Uncle Solo telling all this to Sheed right now?"

"I sure hope so," Mom said. "Knowing my brother, he could've just as likely taken Rasheed to an amusement park and left the dirty work for me to do later."

"Cinda," Dad said, in his you're-being-mean-dear voice.

She gave a *whut-EVER!* shrug.

Otto said, "What do you mean by *dirty work?*"

Dad took this one while Mom cooled off. "Remember how I was saying Mr. Archie had an arrangement with his daughter and son-in-law to keep him afloat? Well, even with him having super rich people in his family, he's looking at a different plan for the future. As we all should."

"Wait," Otto said. "Is this still the analogy, or are you talking about actual Mr. Archie?"

"Actual Mr. Archie."

"How—how do you know what he's thinking about his future?" Otto said. "How do you know *anything* about Mr. Archie?"

"Because we," Mom said, "I mean, *GOO, Inc.*, are trying to save him."

Otto looked to Dad.

Dad said, "By buying his store, and his house, so he doesn't have to worry about money anymore."

"What?" Archie's Hardware had been a part of Fry forever. His house was, like, a mile up the road. Otto forgot all this was supposed to swing back to him, Sheed, and Grandma somehow. Maybe he just didn't want to accept where this was going. But he was a great detective, and all the clues were there.

Mom said, "It's a good arrangement. One we think we can work out for Ma's house, too."

Otto sprang from his seat, notepad and pencil in hand. "Why? Things have been good here! You want to give Grandma's house to your evil bosses."

"Sell." Mom said. "Not *give*."

Dad said, "*Evil* is such a strong word."

"It's been good for you and Rasheed here," Mom said. Serious. "We're glad about that. It's been a strain on us for a long time, though. We've missed being with you, baby."

"I'm not a baby!" It came out harsher than he meant it; Mom cringed. He felt a little bad about that. Still, he needed to say what he needed to say. "Why now?"

Dad said, "Have you ever heard the phrase *waterfront property*?"

"No. What is it?"

"It's a term, in our business, that refers to property that has a view of water. When people can look out their window and see a lake, or river, or the ocean, they're willing to pay a lot more money to live in that place."

"What's that got to do with Logan County? The only water around here is the Eternal Creek, and who wants to look at that?"

Dad said, "You'd be surprised. That's not exactly what we're getting at. There's a term in our business that's new, but quite lucrative."

"You're talking about money, again?" Otto was trying to keep track, but his head was getting swirly.

"A lot of money," said Mom. "That new term is

weirderfront property. Property that's close to *weird stuff*. It's much rarer than waterfront property, and, lately, since we've detected that pulse of energy coming off your cousin, there's a lot more weirderfront property here in Logan County."

Otto's stomach sank. "And GOO, Inc., wants it all."

Dad said, "Exactly! Isn't that exciting?"

12

Black Bean Lemon Drop

THE SKY DARKENED BEYOND the windows of the crowded Riches Brew coffee shop. Sheed and his dad managed to grab a tiny, two-person table as a couple of women in sweatshirts with rolled-up yoga mats tucked under their arms exited with clear cups of icy, creamy drinks in hand.

Sheed caught a snippet of their conversation on their way out: "—girl, I can't believe that Don Glö twist. Who would've thought that—"

Able to plug his ears in time to dodge yet another *Monarch's Gambit* spoiler, Sheed still couldn't find much comfort here. The table they'd taken was in the spot where his favorite booth used to be when this was an ice cream shop. Also, the guy playing his guitar was, like, three feet away and loud.

"How did this change so fast, Dad?" Sheed shouted over twangy chords.

"Blink of an eye, right? I've seen it all over the world. I usually wouldn't spend money in a place like this, but we still need to talk." Dad tilted his chin toward the big bulletin board menu hung high behind the counter. "They have gelato."

"What's that?"

"It's a form of ice cream, a little fancier." Dad waved toward a brightly lit freezer next to the cash register.

Sheed, skeptical, strolled over, wondering if they had his favorite flavor: butter pecan. When he peered through the glass at the vats of colorful, creamy dessert arranged in lumpy mounds, he got even more confused. The tiny cards affixed to each vat said words that might be flavors, but might not, because they didn't seem like anything anyone would want to *taste*.

Honeydew Lavender Kombucha. Black Bean Lemon Drop. Brown Sugar Quesadilla.

Maybe it was a code? Sheed wished Otto was here. He'd know.

"See anything you want?" Dad said.

"No."

"Okay, maybe a beverage, then?"

Sheed looked to the drink menu, and that was just as confusing. "Black Bean Lemon Drop is coffee, too?"

A perky, freckle-faced clerk leaned over the counter, "Welcome to Riches Brew. Anything I can help you with?"

"Can I just have some water?"

"Tap, sparkling, or cucumber-melon?"

"This place is crazy."

Dad yelled from the table. "Tap water for him, large black coffee for me."

When the drinks were ready, Sheed reclaimed his seat at the table while Dad paid. Behind Dad was a blond lady, arms crossed and foot tapping. She was annoyed about something. While Dad gathered their drinks, she pushed up to the counter and said to the clerk, "I need to speak to the manager."

"Is something wrong, ma'am?"

"There's a strange man rolling a grill up the sidewalk toward that beautiful park, and I'm thinking the authorities should be notified."

"That's Mr. James," Sheed said.

"Excuse me?" said Annoyed Lady.

"Mr. James always cooks in the park. His food is good."

"Is that . . . *legal?* Does he have the proper permits?"

"What?" Sheed decided Annoyed Lady was actually *Annoying* Lady.

Dad returned to his seat. "Leave it alone, son."

"But—Mr. James—"

"Is going to be dealing with a lot of that from now on. Trust me, it only gets worse. Which is why it's a good time for us to get out before it gets really bad. You don't want to be here when the art galleries arrive."

Dad sipped his coffee, but Sheed wasn't thirsty anymore. "What do you mean, 'get out'?"

Sheed's dad, with very little preparation or sensitivity to the devastating nature of their new reality, told him about the arrangement the family made in leaving Sheed and his cousin with their grandma and how that arrangement wouldn't last in this version of Logan County that was changing right before their eyes.

Sheed said, "Me and Otto aren't going to live at Grandma's anymore?"

"No."

"So where we going? How's it going to work with the way you and Aunt Cinda fight?"

Dad didn't answer. It was answer enough.

"We—you and me—aren't going to live with Otto, Aunt Cinda, and Uncle DeMarcus? Are we?"

"Probably not, kiddo."

Sheed stood up so fast his chair tipped over, knocking the guitar out of Acoustic Guy's hands.

"Hey!" he said, his voice as off-key as his music.

"What about Grandma? Where's she gonna go?"

"Most likely with your aunt. Sit down."

Sheed shook his head hard enough to fling his Afro pick loose, but his quick reflexes allowed him to catch it before it flew off all wild. "I'm going home. With Grandma. And Otto. I don't care what you say!"

His dad stood too. Slowly. The fingers on one hand spread wide, reaching toward Sheed but stopping just shy of touching him. It confused Sheed because he knew yelling at his father that way, in public, should've made Dad mad. He didn't look mad. He looked scared.

"Son, calm down. You're glowing."

"I'm —" Sheed raised his own hand, noticing the dull yellow luminescence pulsing from his skin.

Everyone stared. Acoustic Guy and some new ladies with yoga mats (how many of them were there?) and Angry Army Truck Guy.

Enough. Sheed stomped past Dad, ready to run all the way home if he had to. Before he reached the door, the coffee shop went dark. A power outage.

Maybe.

Sheed, and the setting sun beyond the shop windows, became the only light sources.

The voice of the perky clerk sounded in the darkness. "Be calm, everyone. I'm sure the electricity will come back on momentarily."

Acoustic Guy strummed a few notes. "Good thing my guitar isn't electric."

Several customers groaned.

With a sudden hum, the lights did return. When they did, there were three new customers in Riches Brew.

The Heads of GOO, Inc., in their matching blazers and colorful turtlenecks, blocked Sheed's path to the sidewalk.

They wore identical smirks, and their heads tilted on the same angle, observing Sheed with a satisfied vibe that made him more uncomfortable than the thought of Black Bean Lemon Drop gelato.

"Well, we've . . ."

"Been looking . . ."

"For you."

Sheed instinctively tensed for a fight.

"Oh, dear, have . . ."

"You tried the . . ."

"Gelato? It's fantastic."

13

Always Unlucky

SOLO, WAY MORE AGILE than he looked, leapt between Sheed and the Heads of GOO, Inc. "I think you want my sister."

The three heads lunged forward, halving the distance between them and Sheed. Their feet weren't touching the ground, though. Their skirts were billowing fabric, undoubtedly meant to disguise this disturbing fact. There was a small, barely noticeable gap between the hem of the skirts and the ground. Did they even have feet? Legs?

How were they standing without them?

"We wanted . . ."

"Your sister . . ."

"To find . . ."

"Something precious . . ."

"For us . . ."

In frightening synchronicity, they said, "SHE FAILED!"

Everyone in the room shuddered.

"But the immense power . . ."

"Coming from the boy . . ."

"Could only stay hidden . . ."

"For so long."

Dad juked left, like he might go that way. When the Heads of GOO, Inc., swayed to block him, he tossed his hot coffee into Ms. Latho's face. All three of the women shrieked, and Dad used the opportunity to grab Sheed's arm and yank him right, sprinting toward the exit.

It almost worked.

There was something like a downed tree wedged through the door, forcing Sheed and Dad to attempt Maneuver #111: hurdles. When they leapt, the tree moved, twisted, coiled around them. Sheed recognized that the patchy pattern wasn't shingles of bark, but scales. Big scales. *Snake* scales.

The muscular reptilian body constricted around Sheed and Dad in two separate loops, not quite painful but not far from it. Sheed's arms were pinned to his side, with some room to work his hands into his jean pockets. Maybe, just maybe . . .

The thickest part of the reptile body twisted in on itself, and with it came the three Heads of GOO, Inc.—the three heads of the snake. Ms. Nyar, Ms. Latho, and Ms. Tep had distinct faces, shoulders, arms, and torsos beneath their tailored coats and fitted tops. But Sheed could now see at some point those deceptively human features tapered into three branches of reptilian flesh that eventually joined a single, slithery trunk.

Ewwwww.

"Let my son go!" Solo yelled, writhing inside his tight reptilian coil. The heads chuckled.

"We imagine that's . . ."

"What your sister . . ."

"Intended when she . . ."

"Lied about the . . ."

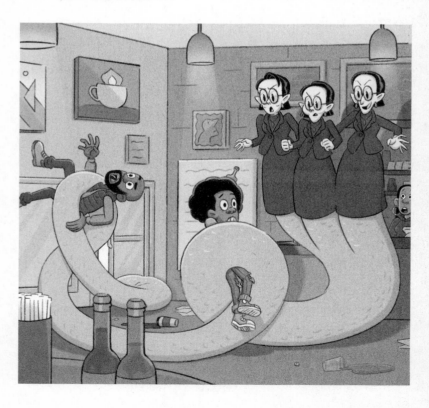

"Source of the . . ."

"Energy we seek."

"That omission will . . ."

"Reflect poorly in . . ."

"Her annual evaluation."

The heads swayed away from Solo to Sheed, each examining a different part of him.

"So . . ."

"Very . . ."

"Curious."

The left and right faces—Nyar and Tep—turned toward the center—Latho—as if conferring.

"So . . ."

"Much . . ."

"Potential."

What kind of potential they thought he had, Sheed wasn't anxious to find out. He'd worked his hand into his pocket and retrieved the thing he'd wanted: a spare Afro pick.

Sheed jabbed the prongs into the scaly flesh.

The Heads of GOO hissed, surprised, in pain. The coils looped around Sheed and Solo loosened, giving them enough room to slip free and run through the exit.

From the sidewalk, Sheed saw that the enormous reptilian body ran a quarter of the way up the block and down a manhole in the center of the street. How far underground the body stretched . . . there was no way to know. Sheed didn't want to think about it too much; he only wanted to get away.

"Come on," Solo said, leading Sheed in the opposite direction, away from the manhole. "We gotta get to the car."

From the corner of his eye, Sheed saw the snake rippling and retracting from the coffee shop. The Heads of GOO were in the open air, a dozen feet off the ground, no longer hiding their true form. Sheed faced forward, running.

They had a clear path on the sidewalk except . . .

Except . . .

Sheed slowed, almost came to a complete stop when he recognized a familiar beast.

Michael Jordan the Goat stood placidly off to the side. From his teeth dangled a white paper bag with the Monte FISHto's logo on it.

Weird, Sheed thought. Then, *What isn't lately?*

The distraction lasted but a second. Sheed remembered where he was going and what was after them; he pushed Michael Jordan the Goat to the back of his mind.

Him and his dad made it to the car. When Sheed tugged on the passenger door handle, there was no give.

"Unlock it, Dad."

Solo's face was all panic. "The keys. I can't find—" He glanced back toward the coffee shop; confusion made his face slack.

Sheed looked back the way they had come. A chill washed over him. The Heads of GOO were nowhere in sight. While the manhole cover lay discarded like a giant penny, nothing occupied the hole itself. Where was the snake?

The street was empty. Anyone who'd been outside made the smart decision to find shelter. Anyone who'd been driving maneuvered their cars to a different route. Solo kept patting his pockets, coming up empty, until he reached in his jacket and sagged with relief. He retrieved the car key from the inside pocket, and clicked the button to unlock the door.

The ground rumbled, forcing them to lurch to one side.

Sheed looked toward the intersection closest to their car. In the center was another manhole. Oh no.

The manhole cover jetted into the air, flipping end over end, before falling and colliding with the asphalt in a clattering crack!

The Heads of GOO rose from the sewer slowly, stretching over Sheed and Solo a good ten or fifteen feet with the confidence of knowing the Alstons would not best them again.

"Nice try, you two. Very . . ."

"Admirable. But now we're going . . ."

"To get down to business."

They loomed over Sheed, clutching at him with their humanlike arms. Victorious.

Until a stranger emerged from the nearby alley.

Dusk had settled over Fry. The strange figure in the

trench coat and fedora peeled himself from the shadows and approached Sheed and the Heads of GOO, fearless. Only one of the heads, Ms. Nyar, noticed him. Her expression was more bemused than anything. The other heads caught on quickly.

"Who . . ."

"Are . . ."

"You?"

The stranger's face remained hidden beneath the brim of his hat, but his accent sounded like the people in those British shows about butlers and maids Grandma watched sometimes. He said, "For now, consider me your travel agent."

The stranger stretched his arms forward. The fingers of his very hairy left hand were splayed, the fingers on his right hand didn't do anything because he didn't have a right hand. There was just an empty, flapping coat sleeve.

He said, "I wish you'd go back where you came from."

The pinky finger on his one and only hand glowed with an amber light, then curled toward the palm with a painful-sounding crack. The same amber light encircled the Heads of GOO. The three faces each displayed a different expression—anger, confusion, and fear—before the entire snake body vanished.

The stranger lowered his arms and took heavy breaths, winded as if he'd sprinted to the battle. "Very good, then."

Solo rounded the car, again placing himself in front of Sheed like a shield. It was a gesture that made Sheed feel funny. He wasn't used to his dad protecting him from anything.

Solo said, "Dude, while we appreciate the assist, I gotta ask the same question that monster did. Who are you?"

The stranger faced them, and when Sheed got a good look at his face, more questions—an infinite number, maybe—came to mind.

"Have you ever heard the story of 'The Monkey's Paw'?" He raised his right arm, where he was missing a hand. Or —er—a paw. "I am the monkey."

14

Lucinda Alston's Biggest Fan

MR. FLUX. THE JUDGE. NEVAN THE NIGHTMARE.

The Legendary Alston Boys of Logan County had faced some bad dudes before, but Otto wasn't sure any of them were as bad as GOO, Inc. Their evil plan wasn't even a secret. They weren't *tricking* anyone. They just gave people money that made them crazy, took the property in exchange for the insanity cash, and their scheme was complete. Sure, you'd think if people knew the money would make them crazy, they might not take it, but, honestly, Otto wasn't so certain.

Then there was Mom and Dad. He didn't know what to make of their reasons for being Employees of Evil. They didn't sound *crazy*.

They sounded *trapped*.

He lay in his bed, staring at the crooked shelves of stuff from his and Sheed's adventures. There was a script page from the time they and the Ellisons got sucked into a campy horror movie. A pair of fuzzy dice from one of Mr. Green's classic cars—the one that sorta came to life and tried to sneak out of town. A small tin of face paint from that mime invasion. All things that helped make property in Logan County weirder than other places, more valuable than other places.

More *home* than other places.

Not so long ago, Otto had worried there'd come a time he'd be in Logan County alone, Sheed gone. Dead. The Black Mirror had relieved the fear of Sheed's death, guaranteeing that Otto and Sheed would live long lives and grow into old, old men. It made Otto relax when he shouldn't have; that reflection of their future was deceptive. Because they'd been *standing together*, Otto had assumed *they'd grow old together*. That promise was never part of the magic that mirror offered.

ENTRY #22

Money means a lot to grownups. They'll trade their house or business for it like Mr. Rickard and Dr. Medina. They'll steal for it if they're bank robbers, even if they might have to go to jail. Or they'll work for monsters who want to buy up the whole county *if . . . if it helps them take care of their families?*

Doesn't working for monsters mean your job will involve doing monstrous stuff, even if you're a good person?

Or were you never good to begin with?

Deduction: Mom and Dad are good. I know it! Grandma taught them to be that way, and they taught me and Sheed. Money may have driven them a little crazy. We'll have to fix that.

Something clacked against the window. Then again. *Clack! Clack!*

Otto feared more Tooth Frogs, but when he saw the shine of a flashlight in the yard below, he slid the window up for a better view. "Wiki? Leen?"

The Epic Ellisons stood by the bushes. Wiki gripping a long-handled light, Leen sporting the same goggles she'd had in class earlier.

Wiki said, "Hey, can you and Sheed come down?"

"Sheed's not here. What's up?"

Wiki crossed her arms, tapped one foot in an annoyed rhythm.

"Wik!" Leen said.

"Fine," Wiki told Leen. To Otto, she said, "We could use a consultation."

Wiki Ellison was asking for his help? Willingly?

It was the best news Otto had heard all day!

"Couldn't handle your were-man case alone, huh?"

Leen got giddy, but Wiki shouted, "No such thing as a were-man!"

Otto grabbed the Legendary Log off the nightstand. "I'm happy to lend my smarts to your investigation. Tell me what you need."

"We analyzed the hair we collected this morning . . ."

"Wait a second." Otto scribbled his most pressing thought.

ENTRY #23

Find out how they're able to "analyze" stuff.

Otto said, "Continue."

"As I was saying, the hair isn't human"—she pointed a finger at Leen, shutting her down before she got started —"not were-man either. It's monkey hair."

Otto frowned. "You said the man spoke to Mr. Lopsided before he ran away."

"I did. Since monkeys don't tend to speak, you see the source of my confusion."

The lenses of Leen's goggles expanded and contracted like owl eyes. In a softer tone, she said, "Sheed told me you two have run into talking animals before. Is that true?"

It was. Nevan the Nightmare and his corrupt Jurors were talking animals. Warped World Dr. Medina. The Spinsters. No monkeys among them, though.

Otto was intrigued, but the more he thought about Warped World and what happened there, the more his mind slipped back to his current problems: his mom and dad wanting to break up the family. His joy at Wiki's need drained away like the last bit of energy in a weak battery.

He closed his log, and said, "Can we talk tomorrow? It's just not a good time."

Wiki spoke to Leen. "See? Told you this was a bad idea. They can't help us."

As down as he was, a bit of Old Otto snapped back into the conversation. "Oh, I guarantee we can help you, Wiki. It's just that my mom's in town, and there's some stuff happening—"

"Your *mom* is here?" Wiki's eyes became the size of tennis balls. "LUCINDA ALSTON IS BACK IN LOGAN COUNTY?"

Before Otto could answer, Wiki jetted around the corner of the house.

"Hey!" Leen said, flipping up her goggles and staring after her sister.

Otto leaned over the windowsill—almost too far; he had to catch himself—to see where she went. Seconds later, the doorbell gonged throughout the house.

Sprinting from his room, Otto was not fast enough to beat Cinda to the door. When his mom opened it, she was greeted by a teary-eyed Wiki, who bounced on her toes and clasped her hands together over her heart.

"Miss Alston? Oh my gosh, oh my gosh, oh my gosh! My name is Victoria Ellison, and I am your biggest fan!"

15

Monkeys Love Seat Warmers

ON THE DRIVE HOME, Sheed and Solo had questions. A bunch! The monkey with the British accent was happy to answer them . . . when he wasn't playing with all the gadgets in Aunt Cinda's fancy rental car.

"Did you know you can control the temperature back here?" He twisted a knob in the seat console, monkey-squealing with delight.

Solo said, "That's not our most pressing concern at the moment."

"Where did you send the Heads of GOO?" asked Sheed.

The Monkey flipped open a hidden cup holder and marveled!

"Sir!" Sheed said.

"None of that sir nonsense. I have not been that since my days in the armed services. You can call me Bernard. I sent that tri-headed beast back to its home office in New York City."

"With a wish?" Sheed said.

"Yes." Bernard waved his hand, where the pinky remained curled. "Monkey's Paw."

Sheed knew this story from school. They read it in language arts class around Halloween last year. It was by a guy named W. W. Jacobs and was about a cursed monkey's paw that granted wishes, but in a messed-up way. Like if you wished for ice cream and got Black Bean Lemon Drop gelato.

Actually, the wishes and the results in the story were worse. Like, wishing-for-someone-to-come-back-to-life-but-having-them-come-back-as-a-possible-zombie worse.

Sheed, not wanting to think about death and zombies, but not being able to stop himself, said, "That story . . . All the wishes turned bad for the people who made them."

"That's because it wasn't *their* paw. I promise you, I've been trying to get it back for decades to avoid all of that nasty be-careful-what-you-wish-for business. It eludes me at every turn. Almost like it enjoys the mischief." Bernard discovered a hidden panel in the ceiling. "Oh, a monitor! Do you have any movies?"

"We don't have any movies!" Solo snapped.

Sheed became instantly annoyed. What right did his dad have to be angry about anything? He was the one who'd spent his sweet time going all over the globe and forgetting to call on birthdays and holidays. When Aunt Cinda and Uncle D would ring up Otto and talk about missing him, Sheed would just fire up the old ThunkleStation and play video game basketball or video game soldier or video game anything to take his mind off knowing better than to expect his own parental call anytime soon. Staring through his window, in serious danger of drifting into a tantrum-level funk, Sheed noticed a man in the distance. Flying.

Not cool flying, like a superhero. More like someone in an invisible stunt plane without a safety harness. Bouncing, and jerking, and dropping, his mouth twisted in screams that were too far away for Sheed to hear.

The flying man banked left, cutting the distance between him and their vehicle in half, putting him close enough to be identified.

Sheed whispered, "Mr. Feltspur?"

He twisted in his seat, pressed his whole forehead to the glass. The old man infamous for flying his strange and varied kites was now the one airborne. What the heck?

Dang fool gonna mess around and get snatched away if a wind gust catches one of them kites wrong.

Grandma been saying that, and there was a kite soaring up and ahead of Mr. Feltspur, dragging the man along. Propelling that kite was the barely visible shape of a familiar disembodied head. Its cheeks puffed, its eyes focused, and its gale-force breath taking poor Mr. Feltspur for the ride of his life.

The Wind banked right suddenly, taking the kite and the man with it, disappearing over the tops of some trees. Gone.

Sheed pressed back into his seat. Horrified.

Solo said, "Since when do they let monkeys into the British Armed Services?"

"Silly, I wasn't always a monkey. I was cursed. When I lost the paw, it became doubly cursed."

"How'd you lose the paw?" Sheed was ready to talk about anything other than what he just saw.

"A rather intense cooking competition. Sadly, I did not win."

"What is happening?" Solo yelled to no one at all.

Sheed whispered, "U-rays."

"Why are you here, Bernard?" Solo asked. "Why did you help us?"

"I was drawn here. I was in the United Kingdom, following yet another lead on my missing paw, when all of a sudden I looked west. Like I'd seen a flash from the corner of my eye and felt a weak tugging at the same time. Every so often, the sensation repeated, like a homing beacon. I decided to investigate. That's the best way I have to paint the picture for you, old chap."

Solo said, "Let me guess. It started about three weeks ago?"

He was looking at Sheed when he said it.

Sheed's stomach twisted. Three weeks ago was Warped World, him taking the Fixityall. So, yeah, all of this was starting to make more sense than Sheed liked.

"Precisely!" said Bernard. "How did—"

The monkey lurched forward, its bright yellow eyes pinning Sheed. "I just felt the tug again. Very strong. It's you, isn't it?"

Sheed picked his 'fro frantically.

Bernard sat back. "Well, then, one query answered.

A host of others sprout up in its wake. Isn't that how it always is?"

"You sound like my cousin," Sheed said. Otto would be excited by a cursed monkey with wish powers. Sheed just felt exhausted by it all.

Solo said, "Okay. You were drawn to my son. Why give us a hand back there? In my experience, there aren't a lot of people — or monkeys — super hyped to jump into a monster fight for strangers."

"It doesn't sound like you've met a lot of great people in your experiences. I'm sorry about that, though I do catch your meaning. Truth is, I didn't do it for you. That was Nyarlathotep. I know its kind, and trust me when I tell you derailing its plans helps me — helps everyone — as much as it helped you in that moment."

Sheed didn't like the sound of that one bit. "Its kind? There are more monsters like that?"

"Of course. What did you think GOO meant?"

Sheed and Solo didn't respond. They didn't know how to.

"They're the Great Old Ones. Evil chaos gods that have existed longer than time itself. Anything they set their sights on is for horrendous and insidious purposes the likes of which you cannot even — Ohhhhh, there's a button back here to make my seat warmer. How cozy."

16
Remind Me Who I Am Again

ENTRY #24

Wiki Ellison is blushing! And being nice.
Because of my mom?

Deduction: If weird is what makes
things valuable in Logan County, this
house has gotta be worth a billion
dollars now.

Wiki and Leen sat at Grandma's table with tall glasses
of grape juice and plates of reheated mac and cheese. Leen
ate and drank heartily while Wiki barely touched hers—
she was too busy rambling to Otto's mom.

"I know about all of your adventures! There was the

time those ninjas tried to heist the Founder's Jewels from the local historical society. The time ninjas tried to put a hypnotizing chemical in the town water supply. The time ninjas tried to take everyone in the county playhouse hostage!" Wiki paused for a breath, then, "You and your brother dealt with ninjas a lot, huh?"

Cinda sipped her tea. "It was the eighties. What can I say?"

"Y'all were the premier heroes of the county when you were our age. Me and my sister wanna be just like you. We've done some cool stuff too. Already have three Keys to the City and about to get a fourth."

Normally, that would've been the moment Otto reminded everyone about the awesome Legendary Alston Boys' adventures—his and Sheed's two keys weren't anything to sneeze at. He just couldn't quite process how much Wiki was gushing over his mom. He'd never seen her like this before.

Leen chewed a mouthful of mac and cheese. "She has a poster of you two on our bedroom wall."

Cinda pushed back in her chair. "There are posters of us?"

Wiki said, "I made one from the old newspaper articles about you they have in the basement at City Hall. I also used those stories to update your Wikipedia page."

"We have a Wikipedia page?"

"Now you do. I mean, I made one for you. A lot of pages get stuff wrong, and that always irks me, so I made sure your page is error free. Kids like us need to know heroes like you exist. We need to know what we can grow up to be. What kind of heroic things do you do now? I couldn't find that in any of my research."

"Ummm." Cinda stirred her tea hard enough to splash the table. "It's complicated."

Wiki leaned forward, cupping her chin in her hands. "I love complicated. Please, tell me. I know it's gotta be epic."

"I . . . well . . ."

Otto, sensing an opportunity (that he was never going to admit Wiki provided), said, "Yeah, Mom. Tell her like you told me. I'm sure she wants to know all about the company you work for."

Cinda focused on her fingernails instead of the little awestruck girl's hopeful anticipation. She scratched lightly at the tabletop. A tic.

Wiki read tics as easily as her sister read science books. A portion of her eagerness fell away. Something was very wrong here, but she didn't know what.

"Mom," Otto said.

"Wiki," Cinda began slowly, the bearer of bad news, "this may disappoint you to hear, but I had to give up adventures a long time ago. Most grownups eventually do. There are responsibilities and tough choices, and . . . and . . . sometimes, you're just not the hero you think you are."

"I don't understand," Wiki said. Words Otto *never* thought would cross her lips. It was a little startling.

Leen's cheeks puffed like a chipmunk's while she spoke and chewed at the same time. "I know what this is." She shoveled another spoonful of mac and cheese into her mouth, interrupting this particular epiphany.

After several seconds of loud, moist chomping, Wiki said, "Sis, what the heck are you talking about?"

Chew. Chew. Chew. "You know how sometimes I'll invent stuff and it doesn't work, or it *really* works and our family has to deal with things like lawsuits and stern warnings from government?"

"Too well," Wiki said, "but go on."

"I get down about it, okay. Mom and Dad say that's the world messing with my confidence, making me forget who I am, and that's why I'm lucky that we're sisters because you remind me that yes, even if my sonic drill was a little too powerful and hit the earth's core, that still means I made a good sonic drill."

Otto said, "Wait. When did that happen?"

Leen spoke directly to Cinda. "What I mean is it sounds like the world messed with your confidence, too. You've forgotten who you are. So you're lucky you met Wiki. If she says you're a hero, then you're a hero, because she doesn't forget anything."

Cinda didn't respond. Though she swiped the back of

her hand across her face, smearing away tears before they fell.

The front door creaked open. Grandma shuffled in, peering over the brown grocery sack in her arms.

Cinda rushed over, still wiping her eyes. "Let me help you with that, Ma."

"I was doing just fine, but thank you." Grandma handed over the bag and noticed they had company. "Victoria and Evangeleen Ellison. How good to see you girls. To what do we owe the pleasure of this visit?"

Leen, still chomping, said, "We came to get Otto and Sheed's help on—"

Wiki kicked Leen under the table.

"Homework."

Otto said, "Because we all know you're way better at your homework when you get our help. Right, Wiki?"

Wiki's smile sharpened. "If you say so."

"Let's go in the living room and look over *the assignment*. I can fill Sheed in when he's back—"

Sheed said, "I'm here."

Grandma had left the door open. Sheed rushed in so fast that had it been closed, he'd have run right through it. Not a good sign.

Solo was close behind.

A one-handed monkey in a trench coat and fedora followed him.

Definitely not a good sign.

Solo said, "Hey, Cinda, your bosses . . . way more evil than we thought."

"Really? You want to fight this out now?" Cinda jerked her head toward the twins. "Can't you see we have company?"

"Not a fight. A fact."

Wiki shrieked, snatching everyone's attention. "OMG! YOU'RE SOLOMON ALSTON!"

Solo said, "Hello?"

Then, a sonic bomb exploded, all the voices and noises combining into audible nonsense. Cinda and Solo yelled at each other. Sheed tried to tell Otto something about gelato, snakes, and black beans. Wiki hyperventilated. Leen pointed her spoon at the monkey, who could talk (he asked if he might sample some of the Southern American delicacy in her bowl). She asked if he was a were-man.

Grandma, over all of it, plugged two fingers into her mouth and blew, piercing everyone's eardrums with a knife-like whistle. "Enough! I swear y'all going to drive my pressure through the roof. Now, one. At a. Time."

Everyone inhaled, ready to speak at once all over again.

Grandma pointed to Sheed. "You, because you look a mess."

Sheed started his story, picking his hair while he talked. "Dad tried to take me to Nice Dream Ice Cream but it wasn't there anymore. There's a new place—"

Cinda's phone double-chirped, an urgent sound. Sheed kept talking while she checked it. Whatever she saw didn't seem so good. She waved her hand in the air, getting everyone's attention. "Rasheed, I'm going to have to interrupt you."

Solo said, "Typical."

Cinda ignored the jab, so Otto knew something was really, really wrong.

His mom had been on the verge of tears before. Now, she looked . . . Otto thought angry at first, and maybe some of that was there, but there was also something like determination on her face. The expression of an Olympian about to attempt an impossible—until it isn't—long jump. She spoke to the room, but her eyes were on Wiki. "Thank you, Victoria. It's fuzzy, but I'm starting to remember who I am now." Then, to Solo, "You're right, my bosses are evil. I will resign in the morning, provided we're all still around."

Grandma used her I'm-concerned-but-trying-not-to-sound-that-way voice. "Lucinda?"

"Okay, okay. Listen." She read directly from the phone. *"Dear loyal employees, we got called back to the home office unexpectedly, but will be returning to the Logan County project by private plane posthaste. In the meantime, we'd like to extend our vast purchasing and deal-making powers to all of you who are still on-site. Please, make any and every effort to acquire as much weirderfront property as possible and turn residents to our cause. Also, there will be a bonus for anyone who can capture one Rasheed Alston. As for the rest of the Alston family, do with them what you will. Sincerely, Ms. Nyar, Ms. Latho, and Ms. Tep."*

Otto said, "We should run, shouldn't we?"

Cinda said, "That would be a yes, sweetie."

17

The Walking Bread

THERE WAS A MOMENT OF INDECISION. A second or two when everyone remained where they were, uncertain that they'd just heard what they heard. Hands were wrung. Mac and cheese was devoured. Loudly.

"What?" Leen asked.

Solo told Cinda, "We need a plan. Maybe the best plan we've ever come up with if Nyarlathotep is as bad as Bernard says. Who's even still in the county that we have to worry about?"

"We can help," said Otto.

Cinda asked Solo, "Remember the team that collected all those toothy frogs?"

Solo mouthed something, ticked off a count on his fingers. "That's, like, nine or ten guys. We can take them."

Sheed said, "We can help."

"That's the *lead* team," said Cinda. "There are several

support teams in town to back them up. So that count's more like forty or fifty."

Solo smacked his forehead. "Then the plan has to be escape. We get out of Logan County fast. If we take Route—"

"WE CAN HELP!" Otto and Sheed said together.

Wiki and Leen joined Otto and Sheed (after Leen got one more spoonful of Grandma's food into her mouth). "So can we."

Cinda and Solo seemed confused, as if the children were speaking an unfamiliar language.

Sheed said, "We can help you plan. If we know what's coming, we can execute our maneuvers."

"Yeah," said Otto, "I've been thinking of ways to fortify the house since the frogs fell. I think—"

"No," Solo said, loud enough to startle Otto.

"Hang on," said Grandma. "The boys are some quick thinkers. Won't hurt to hear them out."

Cinda said, "No, Ma. We're not going to hear them out. It's time—" Her voice had gone high, like it might crack; she forced it down. "It's time we took care of you three like we should've been." To Otto, she said, "You heard your uncle. Now, what I want you to do is go upstairs, pack one bag of things you need. *Need!* Got it? You have five minutes."

Solo told Grandma, "You too, Ma."

Sheed stepped forward. "What about Wiki and Leen?"

"We'll drop them off at their house on our way out

of Logan," Cinda said. "Four minutes and fifty seconds, Rasheed."

Accepting the unyielding countdown, Otto and Sheed ran upstairs while Grandma shuffled up behind them. Otto snatched up his trusty backpack, which stayed loaded with necessities, but—he craned his neck, looking over the entire room.

Sheed dumped dirty, sweaty clothes from a gym bag into a pile on his bed and shoved clean clothes in. He grabbed a few spare Afro picks, some bubble gum, other essentials. In his haste, he noticed Otto's total stillness. "Clock's ticking, cuzzo."

"Do you think we'll be back?"

That froze Sheed, took his mind off which comic books were absolutely necessary for the trip. "I don't know."

They'd slept side by side for years. Called out their maneuvers due to sheer habit, but could probably execute any one of them in perfect synchronicity from the sound of their breathing alone. The Legendary Alston Boys of Logan County weren't two people; they were one team. But for how much longer?

Sheed said, "Your mom told you about what they wanna do."

"And Uncle Solo filled you in."

"He wants to drag me along with him doing whatever it is he does when nobody can find him for months," Sheed said, shaking. "I hate him."

"No you don't," Otto said, horrified. "Grandma says we should never hate anyone."

"Since she's going with you, I guess you'll have to send me any new Grandma wisdom in an email once we've got half the globe between us."

Cinda shouted from the stairs. "One minute."

One minute until they escaped for a night or two? Or one minute until they left the home they knew and loved forever?

Otto and Sheed shared a glance, made some decisions in that moment. Sheed said, "We'll make more time if we have to."

"We've done it before," said Otto.

Cinda wasn't playing. Their time in their room, for now, was almost at an end. They scanned frantically for anything else to cram in their bags. Otto moved first, leaping onto his bed, reaching for the top shelf fastened over it.

Sheed said, "Your mom told us only bring what we need."

Otto grabbed their two Keys to the City of Fry. "Yeah. I *need* to remind Wiki we're just as good as her." He tucked the keys in his backpack a moment before his mom poked her head in, her own bag tucked under her arm. "We're moving. Let's go."

She ushered them downstairs, where everyone gathered in the foyer. Then they all piled into the monstrous rental. Cinda and Grandma up front. Solo and Bernard in the middle row. Otto, Sheed, Wiki, and Leen crammed in the back with all of the luggage piled in the cargo area behind them.

"Seat belts!" said Cinda, though she had the vehicle in motion before anyone was strapped in.

"Easy, there," squealed Bernard. He'd been fiddling with the seat warmer instead of focusing on his safety harness.

At the end of Grandma's driveway, Cinda said, "Girls, quickest way to your house?"

"Left," the twins said together.

Cinda piloted the massive vehicle expertly, and the quiet among the passengers gave the false impression of calm. Otto was freaking on the inside. He kept twisting in his seat like he could still see their home, though it was miles away by now.

Wiki and Leen continued navigating. Mostly Wiki, since Leen had snuck a Tupperware bowl and plastic spoon from the house and continued filling her bottomless stomach with mac and cheese.

Wiki said, "Make the next right onto County Road 7. It shouldn't be long after that."

Cinda did as told, then brought the vehicle to an abrupt stop that made Bernard squeal again.

Ahead of them, in the bright cone of the SUV's headlights, people blocked the road. At least three of them still wore the yellow, full-body hazard suits they'd worn when sucking up Tooth Frogs the night before. The rest — easily twelve or fifteen people — were Logan residents.

Mr. Rickard was among them.

They stood stone still, stared into car's lights without blinking. Even from this distance, Otto could make out the slips of paper tucked sloppily into pockets or clenched in fists.

Checks from GOO, Inc.

The headlights hitting their dollar-sign pupils reflected back money green.

The GOO employees shouted something. The mesmerized county folks became unstuck and shuffled forward, Mr. Rickard in the lead, all of their mouths stretched in silent O's.

Sheed said the terrifying thing they'd all been thinking in some form or another, if not in his exact words, then close enough: "Money Zombies."

18

More Money, More Problems

"BERNARD," SHEED SAID, "WISH THEM AWAY."

"That would be a bad idea."

"Why? You did it to the Heads of GOO."

"Nyarlathotep isn't human. Very low chance of hurting it. If I wish those poor people away, they could very well blink from existence. Or be turned inside out. Or—"

"You said wishes didn't turn bad when you made them!"

"I said they didn't turn bad for *me*. Slight difference."

"Girls!" Cinda said. "Is there another way to get you home?"

She whipped the car around with the Money Zombies a few yards from the bumper, gunned the engine, and rocketed them back into the heart of Logan County, away from the living roadblock. So fast that everyone in the car bounced like Ping-Pong balls; thank goodness for those seat belts.

Wiki, her fingernails digging into the supple leather upholstery, said, "No, ma'am. That was the best way."

"Shoot," said Cinda. "Maybe we can take this thing off-road and just cross one of these fields to get around those, those . . ."

"Money Zombies." Sheed reminded her.

Otto had something unpleasant on his mind. Something that had to be said. "What if they're already at the Ellisons'?"

Wiki's head whipped toward him. Leen finally stopped eating.

Solo gave the Ellisons his ThunklePhone. "Here, call your people."

The girls shook their heads. Wiki said, "We'd rather not."

Leen said, "We're not actually supposed to be out after dark."

Grandma sucked her teeth and mumbled, "The children in this county, I tell you . . ."

Leen snaked a hand into Wiki's bag, retrieved the same gauntlet she'd used to operate her homemade hi-tech goggles in class earlier. She tapped various buttons along the length of the device, generating a series of chiming responses. A robotic confirmation sounded. *Monitoring activated.*

"What did you just do?" Sheed asked.

"Because cases sometimes require us to be outside of our house when we're supposed to be inside of our house, a while back I built synthetic decoys. Our parents and Uncle Percy spend most evenings binge watching stuff on ThunkleFlix, so they're usually satisfied if they catch a glimpse of us from time to time. The decoys will walk past a doorway just as they're looking away. They'll make loud footsteps on the floor above them. Sometimes they'll sing off-key. Stuff that makes them believe we're right where we're supposed to be. It's all good."

"Okay," Solo said, "I have a lot of questions, but the most pressing is what's that got to do with us seeing if they're all right?"

Leen tugged her goggles over her eyes. "In Monitor Mode I can see through my decoy's eyes and check on them that way. No phone call necessary." She bobbed her head, seeing things through her goggles no one else in the car could, while singing a nonsensical, "Doo-doo-doo-DOO-DOO-do-do."

Wiki said, "Well?"

"They're fine. Rewatching last night's *Monarch's Gambit*."

Sheed said, "It was that good they're rewatching already?" He chanced an annoyed glare at the back of Grandma's head.

Without turning around, she said, "Boy, you better get that attitude in check."

Sheed looked away.

Wiki told Leen, "If they're fine, hurry up and put the decoys back on autopilot before Mama, Daddy, or Percy sees them and triggers the countermeasures."

"Chill, Wik. I got this."

Bernard squealed, then asked the obvious question. "What countermeasures?"

Leen said, "Don't sweat it. I promise you, the damage would *not* be permanent."

Solo looked uncomfortable but pocketed his phone. "We'll try to get you back to your family as quickly as possible." He chewed his bottom lip, as if fighting his curiosity. The curiosity won. "Hey, say your people looked at your decoys straight on — not from the corner of their eye — what, exactly, would they see?"

Leen propped her goggles back on top of her head. "Think living mannequins with big baby-doll faces."

"Sweet Lord," Grandma gasped, horrified. She lowered her head in prayer.

Cinda took an out-of-the-way route in attempt to get the girls home before any countermeasures were needed. She went back roads with hairpin turns and bumpy terrain to avoid Fry entirely and escape the county on its opposite side. Only, when they neared the border, that way was also blocked by Money Zombies and hazard-suited GOO workers.

She twisted the wheel and tried a third route. Blocked. Another detour after that — same results. With no clear way to leave Logan, Cinda announced that things were indeed worse than expected. "We're almost out of gas."

Solo said, "Should've gone with a hybrid."

"Shut up," said Cinda.

Otto and Sheed were so, so tired of their parents' bickering. Otto yelled to the front, "I know where we can go to regroup, Mom."

Cinda said, "I think we should find the most remote gas station, and—"

"Listen to the boy!" Grandma's words were soaked in frustration. "For once!"

Cinda's face tightened. Even nearing middle age, she knew better than to talk back to her mom. "Fine. What do you have, son?"

"Well, the first roadblock we ran into, Mr. Rickard was there. I don't think he's going anywhere soon."

Sheed nodded, getting it. "Nice, cuzzo."

Otto finished explaining his very simple plan. "If your bosses are sending workers to buy up everything they don't already have, they probably aren't paying much attention to what they already bought. We should go to Mr. Rickard's house."

#

Thankfully, they were already near the home Mr. Rickard used to own. It was the center house on a short lane, the SOLD sign posted prominently at the edge of the yard. The exterior was bird's egg blue, with a neatly trimmed lawn and wind chimes—a lot of wind chimes—strung from the porch, clinking loudly as everyone exited Cinda's vehicle.

Sheed and Solo spoke at the same time. "We probably shouldn't leave the SUV in the open."

Solo was pleasantly surprised by their like-mindedness. Sheed, annoyed. They both took deep breaths and tried again.

Together they said, "I can pick—"

More surprise, and more annoyance.

"The lock," Sheed finished.

Leen said, "That's freaky."

Sheed stomped to the front door, snatching the lock picks from Otto's hand on the way. Solo stared after him with something like pride. "The apple don't fall far from the tree, huh, Ma?"

Grandma grunted. "So alike, and you don't see the pain that boy's in. You should check your apples more closely."

Solo's proud grin fell away, while the lock clacked open. Sheed ushered everyone inside.

The interior of Mr. Rickard's house was normal. Extremely. They could tell by the framed cross-stitch phrase in the entryway that said *Things Will Be Normal Here, If Nowhere Else.*

No one detected anything to immediately dispute the claim, other than the additional notes placed throughout the house. Some were framed needlework like the one at the entrance (*This Wallpaper Is NORMAL and Does NOT Change Colors with the Seasons*), some neatly written on

Post-its and affixed to things (*My TV Is NORMAL and Does NOT Broadcast Shows from a Dimension Where Everyone Is a Dinosaur*), some hastily scrawled on things with a permanent marker (*My Refrigerator Is NORMAL and Does NOT Replace the Food I Buy with Different Food*). Otto stopped reading them—there were a lot—and found the entry to an empty garage. Inside, he flipped a switch and the outer door rattled up. His mom drove the SUV in.

They regrouped in the living room.

Otto started a new entry in his log. "Mom, since you worked for GOO, you might have the key to how we can beat them. What do you think—"

"Son, stop. Me and your uncle got this. Now, you, Rasheed, and the girls check the rest of the house to make sure there aren't any surprises lurking while the grownups talk."

"And the monkey?" Leen said. "Is he with us, or is he a grownup?"

"I'd wager I'm the oldest one here," Bernard said.

"You look it," said Grandma.

"Dear woman, you wound me so."

Otto was set to argue—about grownups coming up with a plan on their own, not Bernard's age—but Sheed grabbed his sleeve and tugged him toward the back rooms. "Don't bother. They don't listen to us anyway."

Wiki and Leen followed the boys room to room, the

"grownup talk" from the front of the house nothing but indecipherable mumblings in the background. Which also meant the grownups couldn't hear them.

Wiki said, "This is bad."

Leen said, "I know, I left my food in the car."

"Not what I meant, sis." To Sheed, she said, "Why'd you call those people Money Zombies? What's GOO, Inc., doing to the county?"

In a bad mood, with no desire to talk, Sheed motioned to Otto and his Legendary Log, and Otto gladly recited things he'd been writing down all day. He talked while they searched under Mr. Rickard's bed, behind his dresser, in his bathroom, finding that everything was normal. All the Post-it notes said so.

"So," said Leen, recapping. "Sheed's emitting some sort of weird energy called U-rays because of medicine he took on the other side of a Warped World mirror. That energy is attracting all sorts of weird stuff to the county." To Wiki, she said, "Which explains Bernard the talking monkey who is not a were-man."

Wiki said, "Now Otto's Mom's company—which is evil—wants to buy all the land because it's weird and that will make them a bunch of money?"

Otto said, "Basically."

"THERE'S NOTHING BASIC ABOUT THAT, OTTO!" Wiki said.

They moved from Mr. Rickard's bedroom to his home office. There was a whiteboard mounted to the wall similar to the one in their classroom, a desk with a powered-down computer, and a bookshelf filled with volumes on science and technology. Also a worktable, with the oddest item they'd run across in the self-proclaimed normalcy of the house so far.

It was boxy, with knobs and gauges and a springy cord stretching from an audio jack to, well, it seemed something like a microphone, but not exactly.

"What is this?" Sheed asked.

"A CB radio," Leen answered.

Wiki said, "Our uncle Percy has one that he uses to talk to his trucker buddies when they want company on the road. It's old school."

As indicated by a Post-it note affixed to the top of the device: *This Radio Is Normal Because It's Actually Normal . . . Radio waves apparently work exactly as they're supposed to in this county. Thank Goodness!*

Wiki sat on the stool before the table, turned the power knob, lighting the gauges and triggering a static squelch before the signal clarified into random chatter. Otto identified a second Post-it labeled *Frequently Used Channels*. He pointed at the one marked *City Hall*. "Try that."

Wiki worked the tuner.

Leen, her attention on Sheed, touched his arm,

something that normally triggered at least a half smile and blush. Not that time. "You don't seem okay."

"Our parents . . . they want to split us up. Or split me up . . . I don't know. I'm pretty sure Grandma's going with him." He jabbed a thumb in Otto's direction and clenched his jaw.

"What?"

Otto overheard the conversation but forced his focus on Wiki and the radio. Sheed needed to get it off his chest his own way.

"Me and my dad, we've barely talked . . . I don't even know him like that, but he's all of a sudden going to take me with him bumming around the world? It's so stupid, it makes me wonder if him and my aunt have really thought about this or they're just making dumb grownup decisions like the people selling out to GOO and going crazy over the money."

Leen said, "He told you that today? It's definite?"

"He told me today, but I'm not going to let it be definite."

Otto couldn't resist, because it sounded so ominous—he had to ask. "What's that mean?"

A familiar voice sounded through the CB speakers before Sheed could answer.

"*This is Mayor Ahmed from the town of Fry in Logan County, Virginia. I'm broadcasting on this frequency because nothing else is working. Not our phones. Not our computers. If*

150

you're out there and you can hear me, either seek shelter or come to City Hall to help us deal with all this . . . all this . . . weirdness. If you do come to us, be forewarned . . . Do not take money from men in strange suits and do not eat the gelato! Your very sanity may depend on it!"

19

The Monkey Said Be Careful
What You Wish for, More or Less

WIKI THUMBED THE TALK BUTTON at the base of the microphone. "Mayor Ahmed, this is Wiki Ellison. Me and my sister are with the Alston Boys. Over."

"Yes, yes, yes!" The mayor said, perhaps through . . . tears? "We could really use your assistance. Can you get here? Over."

"Can we?" Wiki asked the room.

Before anyone spoke, Leen's control gauntlet emitted a rapid, urgent beeping. She frowned and pulled her goggles over her eyes. With the lenses activated, some kind of audio link turned on, too. Standing so close to Leen, Sheed heard a thin sound that was something like a woman shrieking.

"Uh-oh," Leen said.

Wiki, expressionless, said, "You forgot to turn off Monitor Mode."

"I forgot to turn off Monitor Mode."

Low, but crisp, Otto heard the girls' uncle Percy yelling, "*What are those?*"

Otto said, "They see your decoys?"

"That's putting it mildly." Leen tapped buttons on her wrist. Then, presumably to the decoys, she said, "Deploy countermeasures."

An instant later, light flashed around the rim of the goggles, a pulse strong enough to brighten the entire room for a microsecond. Things got quiet at the Ellison house.

Sheed said, "What just happened?"

"A specific pattern of light shot from our decoys' eyes, temporarily blinding everyone in our house and triggering instant sleep. They'll be snoozing until morning."

Wiki said, "When they wake up, we're going to be in big trouble, Leen."

"I know." Leen was way perkier than any sane person should be under the circumstances. So, typical Leen. "We got nothing to lose now, right? Tell the mayor we're in. What about you guys?"

"Getting past our parents and Grandma's going to be tricky," said Otto, considering options and maneuvers.

Sheed jerked forward, reached past Wiki, and smashed the CB talk button. "We'll be there, just hold tight. Over." He twisted the power knob to the Off position. "Let's go."

"How?" said Otto. "My mom . . . your dad . . . Grandma."

"Leen's decoys gave me an idea."

"A new maneuver?"

"Not exactly."

Sheed made his way toward the living room, their little group trailing. The grownups were in yet another heated debate. Cinda made jerky motions with her hands for every word she uttered until she noticed Sheed round the corner. Solo's shoulders slumped. "Son, I thought we told you—"

Sheed said, "Bernard, what's that on your sleeve?"

The monkey lifted his arm, unsure what he was looking for. His paw was exposed.

Sheed grabbed him by the wrist and said, "I wish all of the grownups would go to sleep and dream great dreams until we actually need them."

"Nooo," Bernard began just as his hand glowed with mystical energy. His ring finger curled inward, wish granted.

Solo went wide-eyed, stretching for his son like he could undo what had just been done. His heavy eyelids slammed shut, and he collapsed on the floor. Cinda went limp on a love seat. Grandma flopped on the couch. Bernard was the last to go down, fighting, and losing, against his own magic. "What have you done?"

"What we should've been doing all along. Handling this ourselves."

Bernard shouted a primate squeal, then fell next to Solo. Snoring.

Otto grabbed Sheed by the shoulders. "Are you crazy? The wishes could go bad."

"I was very specific. They'll sleep until we need them. It should be fine."

Wiki said, "What if you never think you need them?"

Doubt shadowed Sheed's face, but he'd committed them to this now. "We'll check on them in the morning. Now we do what we're good at." He pointed at Otto. "We're Legends." Then to the girls. "You're Epic. Maybe if we show them what we mean to this county, they'll know how dumb it is to mess it all up."

Otto said, "I actually agree with this part of the plan."

"Then that means there's definitely a way we can improve it," said Wiki, "We're in."

"Let's go get Logan back from GOO!" Sheed burst through the front door and into the night.

A bemused Otto said, "I thought I was the one that made good speeches."

They were on their way.

#

Mr. Rickard's house was a couple of miles from City Hall. Bikes would've been so clutch, but Otto figured there might be some benefit to cutting through yards and staying off the road. They hoofed it, slinking between houses at a good pace with a mild breeze at their backs. Midway through the trip, they encountered a group of Money Zombies lumbering along the road leading into town, each gripping a GOO, Inc., check. Hunkering down in some shrubs, they let the zombie herd pass. Once it was all clear, they resumed the trek, the breeze a consistent gust now, pushing them along.

Leen said, "I feel weird leaving your parents and your grandma back there like that."

"Weirder than you felt leaving your parents in a trance?"

"Yeah. I know what my decoys do, you don't know what monkey paw magic does."

Was this their first fight?

Sheed only shoved his hands in his pocket, refusing to argue. Truthfully, he wasn't feeling great about what he'd done, either. He'd been mad, and sure, sometimes his anger got the best of him. Usually that meant a tantrum. Not, well, not what he did back at Mr. Rickard's.

Otto kept sneaking glances his way. Sheed sped up on purpose, knowing Otto would keep pace; it put some private conversation distance between them and the Ellisons.

Sheed said, "Go on, say it."

"Say what?"

"I went too far."

"Eh."

"What's 'eh' mean?"

"Mom and Uncle Solo aren't good listeners. They don't even listen to Grandma. I didn't know not listening to Grandma was an option. And"—this part was hard for Otto to admit—"even if they had reasons to do it, my mom and dad working for evil people isn't a good look. They, maybe, *needed* a time-out."

"Don't feel too bad. My dad just sorta wandering the earth isn't a whole lot better. If he helped more, your mom and dad maybe could've done something different. Why you lookin' like that?"

Otto made a face he didn't mean to make.

"Cuz!"

"I know we don't really remember your mom, Sheed, but he does. I think when she got sick and died, it really messed him up. That sort of thing might get someone to make not-great decisions. *I* made not-great decisions when

157

I thought you were going to die. I stole that medicine in Warped World and didn't care about the side effects or consequences. Now look at us. Look at Logan County."

Sheed shook his head. "I *took* the medicine knowing *something* could happen. Neither of us thought it would be this." He swept his hand in the general direction of City Hall.

"That's what I mean," Otto said. "I don't think Uncle Solo knew what leaving for so long would do to our family. To you."

"Well, he should've."

"If we get through this GOO stuff, do you think all the county folks, and everyone in Fry, will say the same thing about us? We should've known better?"

Sheed didn't have a good answer.

Otto felt guilty and uncomfortable. Also, afraid. They were making progress, but slowly. In the time it took them to reach City Hall, how many more of their neighbors were being turned into Money Zombies?

They couldn't do anything until they talked to the mayor. At this pace, they were still ten minutes away from the Hall. Otto took the opportunity to get some notes down:

ENTRY #27

The Legends and the Epics are at it again! But . . .

158

What if this is our finale? The end
of the story here in Logan County.
If I'm being honest, that scares me
more than Nyarlathotep and GOO, Inc.,
and all the Money Zombies in the
world. We've faced off against the
weird and scary a bunch. I think we
have a great chance at saving the
day. When we're on the other side of
this fight, can we save what we have
here? Us all being friends and having
each other's backs (even when we're
competing for keys)?

If our parents do what they say
they're going to do . . . I don't think
so.

Deduction: So, even if we win, we lose.

For the first time ever, he found no satisfaction in a
sound deduction.

20

You've Got a Friend in . . . Windy?

THEY FINALLY MADE IT into Fry city proper, with the night temperature dropping low enough to see their breath. Breath that got yanked from their mouths and whisked away on the steady gusts at their backs. Given how chilling all the strangeness they'd been encountering was, the town hardly needed any help from the evening breeze. There was one small group of Money Zombies being led by GOO employees that they avoided easily (though the boys were horrified to see Mr. Lopsided from the Lopsided Furniture Company had joined their ranks). More terrible was how the city itself had changed.

Just as Nice Dream Ice Cream had become Riches Brew, other familiar businesses had changed in the blink of an eye. Dr. Medina's Veterinarian Office was now something called Animal Mart: A GOO, Inc., Company. The local newspaper, the *Logan County Gazette,* was now the *New County Times: A GOOspaper.*

Something that hadn't changed: the towering neon fish in the sky blazoned with Monte FISHto's name and its proclamation of over a billion served. Otto's eyes were drawn to it, and, for reasons he didn't understand, he was comforted, if only for a moment.

"You ready?" Sheed said.

Otto evaluated the final route to City Hall. "I don't know. Something feels off. Maybe we should wait."

A mighty gust of air smacked Otto in the back, knocking him completely from his hiding place.

"Oh no," said Sheed. "Not you."

Otto peered into the alley shadows, almost missing the faint outline of the head.

Wiki stated the obvious. "The Wind is back."

The disembodied head hovered over a dumpster, its unblinking eyes slowly panning from the boys to the girls, then it rotated sideways, showing off its profile. It looked like someone trying to whistle casually and avoid notice. If it had a full body, it would've been stuffing its hands in its pockets and pretending to be occupied kicking rocks.

"What are you doing?" Sheed said. "We see you."

Still in profile, its eyes cut back toward them. There was a strong, *Who? Me?* vibe to it. Then it faced the opposite direction, like it might make a run for it.

"Wait," Wiki said. "Don't go."

"Why are you telling it not to go?" Sheed had a horrible flashback to a skybound Mr. Feltspur disappearing over a forest. "It should definitely go."

Wiki spoke to the wind but pointed at Sheed. "Are you following him?"

"It's not following me."

"Are you?" Wiki asked the Wind again.

It faced them, looking guilty as all get out, then bounced in the air. A motion Otto interpreted as a nod. It was hard to tell, since it didn't have a neck.

"Why?" Wiki asked.

It bounced high, then settled in its original position. A shrug maybe? Hard to tell, because it had no shoulders.

"Are you drawn to his U-rays?"

Another bounce, but jerky. Seemed like it might be confused. Otto interpreted this particular gesture as *What's a U-ray?*

"Stop asking it questions about me!" Sheed insisted.

Wiki said, "No. Here's why . . . If you're still emitting those U-ray things you told us about, and it's drawing the Wind to you, what else is going to get drawn to you? The GOO guys? The Money Zombies?"

Because it was Wiki, Otto's automatic response was to argue, but he stopped short because she had a point. Sheed's silence suggested he understood it, too.

Leen had her goggles on, scrutinizing the elemental. "Is there something you want from Sheed?"

Another shrug bounce. Was that a maybe?

When it wasn't trying to blow their faces off, it had the demeanor of a cute and bashful animal—the kind you saw in ThunkleTube videos. Like the one where a walrus played peekaboo with a baby. Otto loved that walrus.

"You're not here to hurt us?" said Otto.

The Wind shook side to side: *no.*

"Well, that's something."

Wiki said, "Look, we gotta go over to City Hall. Can you wait here for us? We'll try to figure what your deal is when we're done."

The Wind's eyes narrowed. It looked to Sheed, one eyebrow arched high.

Sheed said, "I swear we won't forget."

Before they left the alley and the Wind behind, Leen asked, "Can we call you Windy?"

Bounce-bounce. *Cool.*

Leen nodded back, satisfied.

They moved silently, using the shadows to conceal them, making it all the way to the Hall's main entrance before meeting an obstacle in the form of a familiar face. Inside the double glass doors, wielding a golf club, was Wallace, an old schoolmate who was now just old due to an unfortunate accident down at the Eternal Creek. The cursed waters of the creek made Wallace age about twelve years in a single afternoon, so he had to do grown-up stuff like work at City Hall and accounting. And, apparently, guarding the Hall from a Money Zombie attack.

"Wallace," Otto whispered, glancing over his shoulder afraid of being spotted. "Let us in."

Wallace did not turn the thumb lock on the double doors. "How do I know you're still you?"

Sheed said, "Everyone who's turned got money first, and their eyes look like dollar signs." He pulled his pants pockets inside out so they hung at his hips like bunny ears, then made his eyes bulge so Wallace could check his pupils. "We're kids, and we're broke."

"Now that you mention it, you do look broke." Wallace turned the lock, shoved the door open. "Come in."

He motioned them inside, pulled the door shut behind them, and turned into a vibrating bundle of worry. "Where are you coming from?"

"Mr. Rickard's neighborhood," Otto said.

"Did you see any of them? Did they offer you a deal?"

Sheed said, "We did, but we either ran or hid."

"Good. Do you know some people are actually going out *to find* those GOO goons? When things started going bad, I tried to offer Mr. Wilson—owns the pawnshop on the edge of town—shelter, and he said I was stupid and should be trying to get some of that weirderfront money."

Wallace shook his head slowly. "I don't know that I ever liked Mr. Wilson much. Come on."

Now that Wallace knew they hadn't been turned by GOO, he brightened significantly, eager to escort them deeper into City Hall. They crossed the marble-tiled lobby, their sneakers mouse-squeaking and Wallace's sensible grownup shoes clopping with every step. Their path took them past several offices where city employees huddled in corners and under desks, quaking at the sounds of people they didn't recognize. One worker, mostly hidden in the shadows, had taken a decorative flagpole as a spear, prepared to poke any oncoming danger. When he recognized them, he burst into grateful tears and stepped into the light.

"Oh, thank goodness! It's the Legendary Alston Boys and the Epic Ellisons! We're saved."

Otto, Sheed, Wiki, and Leen frowned, peered, gasped, and chuckled respectively, recognizing the uniform, if not the man himself.

Otto said, "You're . . . *the sheriff?*"

"Yes. Yes I am."

None of them had ever seen the man before.

He was pear shaped, with an unruly mustache and bushy brown hair. His uniform was tan with brass buttons, and his badge looked like a toy. For all the good he did around town, it might as well have been.

Wiki said, "You've been hiding? In here? With the rest of the city workers?"

"Exactly. I don't know if what's happening out there is exactly *illegal*—which means it wouldn't necessarily be in my jurisdiction. Figured hey, let me ensure this building is secure."

Leen said, "Do you plan to stop hiding—I mean, *making sure the building is secure?* And do something more helpful?"

"Do I have to?"

Sheed said, "Probably best you stayed put."

"Precisely what I wanted to hear. Love your work, by the way." He saluted them and backed into his gloomy hutch.

"All righty, then," said Otto. "Can we see Mayor Ahmed now?"

Wallace said, "No problem."

They climbed the stairs to the mayor's office, leaving the safety and security of the first floor to the not-so-brave sheriff. Felt harmless enough, except for one thing . . .

No one checked to see if Wallace had relocked the front door.

#

Mayor Ahmed's assistant, Miss Mendez, greeted them in the reception area outside the mayor's office with another golf club cocked and ready to swing. She relaxed at the sight of the children. "The mayor's been waiting on you!"

She pounded on his polished mahogany double doors with a rhythmic knock that sounded like a code. The brass mail slot in the door flipped open at waist level. Everyone knelt to peek through the opening into Mayor Ahmed's dark eyes. "Good, it really is you."

The slot closed. Everyone straightened to their full height and waited to the sound of several locks unlatching. After the eighth lock, one half of the double doors swung inward, granting the Alstons and the Ellisons entrance.

They stepped inside, and Mayor Ahmed said, "Thank you, Wallace. Return to your post. Mendez, keep trying the CB and let me know if there are any changes to the situation."

The mayor resealed the doors and redid the locks.

Otto and Sheed, and Wiki and Leen had all been in Mayor Ahmed's office before when dealing with the various threats that had struck Logan County and the City of Fry specifically. The mayor's childhood fishing rod was still mounted on the wall across from his desk, next to a picture of a bass he'd reeled out of the Eternal Creek when he looked about Otto and Sheed's age—the bass was, literally, as big as the mayor because, well, it was the Eternal Creek. Then there was the indoor flagpole with the Virginia state flag and the American flag hanging limply from it in the far corner. The mayor's personal dual slushie machine hummed with blue and red sugary goodness swirling in the glassed-in cylinders. Usually, a blue slushie would've been Otto's first priority, but given the more important issues at hand, he could wait a bit before partaking. Maybe he'd get a to-go cup.

"Please, sit," said Mayor Ahmed.

Never had both teams visited on a joint mission. The problem with this became clear immediately. There weren't enough chairs.

The mayor circled to his side of the desk. All four heroes moved for their usual seats at the same time, causing a collision of shoulders and elbows. They gathered themselves quickly, then Otto and Sheed took a step backward. Sheed said, "Grandma taught us to make sure ladies have seats before we get comfortable."

Leen gushed, "Thank you, Sheed."

When she went to sit, Wiki grabbed Leen's arm and hauled her back up. "*We were taught* that we don't have to entertain patriarchal traditions."

Sheed said, "Huh?"

Otto wrote down:

Look up <u>patriarchal.</u>

Wiki rolled her eyes. "Oh, never mind. My feet hurt from all the sneaking, so just this once I suppose it's fine."

She allowed Leen to sit, then plopped in the remaining chair.

Mayor Ahmed said, "This company—this—this GOO —really blindsided us, kids. They're buying up things so fast, changing the very face of who and what we are. I'm afraid if we don't act quickly, Logan County will barely be recognizable by this time tomorrow. We should talk about your role, and the Keys to the City."

Given how serious the situation was, Otto felt almost ashamed to be discussing Keys to the City. Almost. "Well, you know you can always count on the Legendary Alston Boys to get the job done. Even though this would mean a *third* key for us, I promise that Logan County is always our *first* priority."

Sheed said, "Wow. That was really smooth, cuzzo."

Wiki sprang from her chair. "Oh no. The Epic Ellisons are clearly the best choice for solving the problem. While our *fourth* key would be appreciated, it's certainly not a requirement for doing *the right thing*. Don't you agree, sis?"

"Don't drag me into y'all's mess," Leen said.

Mayor Ahmed's gaze bounced between them, flustered. "What are you talking about? I can't give you any more keys."

Otto, confused, said, "Sorry, Mayor. Is there a limit on how many keys can be awarded? If so, it must be three because they have three, and that means if there's a key in this at all, it should automatically come to the Legends in the room."

Wiki started up. "Oh please, Otto. If we're all helping, how could you possibly get a key and we don't? That doesn't make any sense."

"It does make sense if you Epics peaked early and got an extra key before you really deserved it. Not saying you don't have sound judgment, Mayor Ahmed."

"Children!" the mayor said. "Stop. There's no limit, there just aren't any more. I gave them all to you for safe-keeping—one for every time you proved yourselves worthy protectors. Now's the time to use them."

Sheed said, *"Use them?* I thought they were, like, trophies."

"No! Those are *Keys to the City!* They unlock Fry, and all its potential. Which is what we'll need if we have any hope of saving our town and county."

Confused, slow blinking from all.

The mayor said, "Sorry, was I not clear about that before?"

21

The Cha-Ching Mob

OTTO REMEMBERED THE FIRST TIME Mayor Ahmed gave them a Key to the City.

It was after the whole Laughing Locust thing. He'd sat them down in this very office and told them, "You should have this. For the good of the town."

Sheed, mesmerized by the clacking silver ball thing on the mayor's desk, had barely paid attention. You know, the contraption where you pull back one silver ball hung from a string, then let it go and it strikes four other silver balls, but only the ball on the other side pops out from the force. Then, when it comes back, the same thing happens on the side you started with. Back and forth, back and forth, back and—

Otto shook himself from his trance and found Sheed playing with those silver balls again. He snapped a finger in front of his cousin's eyes, "Hello?"

"Sorry," Sheed said.

Leen stroked his hand. "It's the little things that get you, huh? You should probably focus now."

Otto removed their two keys from his backpack and laid them on the mayor's desk. He'd framed them, never, ever suspecting they had a purpose beyond boasting. "These are for actual locks?"

"Yes," said the mayor.

Otto asked Wiki, "Where are yours?"

The twins reached beneath their shirts, revealed silver chains from which the keys dangled. One on Leen's chain, two on Wiki's. Leen said, "We always thought they were cute accessories."

Wiki scowled.

"Well, *I* always thought they were cute accessories."

"Oh dear." Mayor Ahmed ran his hand down his face like a squeegee, as if trying to wipe away his panic. "I'd been meaning to sit you all down and explain the history of those keys. I was just always so busy running this wacky town. One crisis after another."

Sheed said, "Seems like now would be the time."

"You're familiar with our town's founder? Fullerton French Fryer was a teacher who came to Logan County over two hundred years ago with a group of settlers. Originally, the township formed around a tiny schoolhouse and the wagons they rode in on. The city grew and grew, eventually becoming the foundation of what we live in today.

What Fullerton and his people built up from grass and mud was the first example of the town's potential being unlocked.

"Fullerton's son, Frederick, wanted to make sure there was never a time when the town's potential couldn't be called forth in its greatest time of need. He created five locks and five keys, to be used in case of emergency." The mayor rose from his chair. "I think this is the emergency."

Otto said, "Is the town's potential like magic? Something that will give us power to fight GOO, Inc.?"

"Sounds that way, doesn't it? I can't tell you for sure because none of the town's history describes what, exactly, Fry's potential is. No emergency has been big enough to warrant such action. Until now."

Sheed said, "So where the locks?"

"I don't think I'm supposed to tell you," the mayor said, pacing to the window and peering out. "There's something in the town archives about adhering to 'Quest Rules.' All that seems very tedious to me, and I don't think we have much time to muck about. Yes"—his neck swayed, as if searching for something beyond the glass—"I'm going to skip all of that."

Miss Mendez's rhythmic knock pounded on the other side of the doors. Mayor Ahmed shuffled over to answer and told the kids, "Just one moment."

The mayor crouched and popped his mail slot. "What's going on, Mendez?"

"A Fry resident brought you an important note," Mendez said. Her voice sounded funny. Almost mechanical.

"Well, let's have it."

The folded slip of paper poked through the mail slot. It was a familiar shade of green Otto recognized a moment too late, "Mayor Ahmed, no, it's a—"

But, because it came from someone he trusted, the mayor took the GOO, Inc., check with no hesitation.

Upon grasping the paper, the mayor stiffened as if the check were electric. When he faced them again, the worry from before had fallen off his face. Now he wore a content expression, the expression of someone who'd seen the error of their ways through their new dollar-sign pupils. "Oh, goodness. What was I saying before?"

Wiki and Leen shuffled backwards. Sheed nervously gripped his Afro pick. Otto swept their Keys to the City back into his backpack.

"You were gonna tell us where to find the locks for our keys," Sheed said, hopeful.

"I was, wasn't I?"

Instead of giving them the answer they so desperately needed, Mayor Ahmed began undoing the locks on his door, eight in total. He started with the top one. Beyond the door, the loud shuffling of many feet. Had everyone else in the building been turned into Money Zombies by GOO?

Probably.

They were trapped by all those new zombies, with only seven — now six — locks keeping them safe.

"We gotta get out of here," said Otto.

"Of course we do," said Wiki. "Y'all got a maneuver for this?"

Otto eyed the flagpole in the corner. "Kinda. You're not going to like it."

Sheed saw where Otto was going. "Maneuver #72?"

"Yep."

Leen beamed! Her excitement was a little disturbing. "We're going to do something dangerous, huh?"

Mayor Ahmed undid the fifth and fourth locks.

The boys ran to the flagpole, unclamped the Virginia state flag and the American flag. Otto handed the state flag to Wiki and Leen. "Grab the corners and stretch it out."

Wiki's voice cracked. "What is Maneuver #72?"

"*The paratrooper.*" Sheed motioned toward the window overlooking the town square.

"No way!"

"We can't go the way we came in," Otto said, stomach churning. Mayor Ahmed only had two locks left, and the double doors rattled with the heavy pounding from the Money Zombies on the other side. There was also the moaning. An unnerving sound that they hadn't been close enough to hear before. A low bass utterance of "Cha-Ching. Cha-Ching."

Wiki stressed her point. "It's not going to work. Tell them, Leen."

"Well, the strength of the flags is questionable. Are they sturdy enough to support our weight? Possibly. The biggest problem is we aren't going to be up high enough. Parachutes —real ones—need to be opened at a certain height so they have time to slow you down. That's time we don't have when we're jumping from the second floor. If we jump out that window holding these flags, we're probably going to break something. Then we won't even be able to run from those things outside."

Otto could not deny the logic.

Sheed, though, with all the weirdness he'd drawn to Logan County, had given up on logic after he'd read the words *Black Bean Lemon Drop*. Mr. Feltspur and his runaway kite came to mind. "If we can't parachute down, how about we glide across?"

Mayor Ahmed was down to his last lock. No more time to explain. Sheed leaned out the window, whistled as loud and as sharp as he could, then shouted, "Windy! We need you now!"

The roar was immediate and startled the mesmerized mayor. He fumbled with the last lock, while the papers on his desk took flight like leaves in a tornado.

Windy bobbed outside the mayor's window.

Otto told Wiki, "I'm not sure if it would be patriarchal to let you two go first, but—"

The Money Zombie horde obliterated the final lock plate, spraying splinters across the floor and spilling inside, checks tightly gripped.

Wiki and Leen took the Virginia flag between them and pushed past the boys. Wiki said, "We'll discuss the patriarchy and your problematic role in it later."

They leapt into open air, but Windy kept them aloft with a powerful gust. The twins stayed airborne, dangling from their respective ends of the flag/kite/parachute, and sailed slowly toward the other side of Town Square.

The herd rushed Otto and Sheed, forcing them to make

the leap without proper preparation. A problem, since their American flag was twisted and couldn't catch the wind. The boys dropped like stones.

They screamed, waited for the inevitable painful impact . . . that didn't come.

Windy zipped back to them, descended faster than they fell, and blew a cool cushion of air that caught them like a pillow an inch before hitting the ground. Then Windy stopped blowing, and their butts smacked the concrete. Bruised, but unbroken.

They stood, looked at the flag between them. Sheed said, "Windy, would you mind giving this back to the mayor?"

The elemental blew the flag up toward the second floor, guiding it with precision that probably came from centuries of being a living force of nature. Mayor Ahmed and the other Money Zombies had leaned out the window peering at the boys, and Windy draped the flag over them like a net.

On the sidewalk before the Hall's main entrance, a second group of Money Zombies—their friend Wallace in the lead—spotted them and lumbered their way.

The boys raced across Town Square to Wiki and Leen. Wiki said, "Now what?"

They could run and keep running, Otto supposed, but how long was that going to last? They'd bet a lot on going to the mayor. A bet they lost.

The Money Zombies from the Hall were heading

toward them. Worse, Sheed spotted a second herd coming from another direction. They had limited options.

They tried Archie's Hardware first, one of the few Main Street businesses that hadn't been bought and converted into something GOOier yet, but it was dark and locked. Otto thought briefly of trying their Keys to the City, but recognized they weren't skeleton keys capable of unlocking everything in town.

Wiki said, "What now, Otto? We can't stay on the street like this."

"You mean you don't have any Epic ideas?"

"I don't. I'm sorry. Not this time."

That she answered so honestly, without taking any sort of jab at Otto, made him more scared than he'd been the whole night. They really were in trouble.

"Leen?" Otto said.

She shook her head. "I don't have a gadget for this."

Sheed wandered further down the sidewalk, staring into the distance at nothing. Or so Otto thought.

Leen pointed Sheed's way, seeing what he saw. "Whose goat is that?"

Michael Jordan the Goat, with the ever-present bag of fast food clamped in his teeth, scratched one hoof on the concrete and jerked his horned head. A clear come-on gesture.

Wiki said, "I think the goat wants us to go with him.

It's not even the fifth weirdest thing I've seen today. What do you think, Mr. U-rays?"

Sheed said, "Why not?"

Michael Jordan the Goat galloped. They followed.

Leen said, "You guys know where it's taking us?"

Otto said, "I think I do."

The Monte FISHto's mascot, rimmed in neon, sat high in the sky. A beacon of light, drawing them close. Perhaps a safe haven.

Then Otto had a grim thought: bugs probably thought the same thing before they flew into the zapper.

22

Quest Rules, Though?

SHEED THOUGHT THE HIGH, BRIGHT Monte FISH-to's sign was like a star in an otherwise dark cosmos, a sign of possible safety. Almost blinding white light beamed from inside the restaurant—everything seemed to be glowing, from the tables to the countertop to the stainless-steel grills. As comforting as this beacon should've been, an eerie sensation fell over Sheed. The parking lot was empty. There were no customers—maybe because it was getting late, almost eleven o'clock (*And well past your bedtime,* the Grandma in his head said). Yet there was something more to the hesitance Sheed felt. It was Dr. Medina's whole "U-ray" thing, him being a magnet for the uncanny. Whatever was pulling weird things like Windy to Logan County, Sheed wondered if it felt something like the tug drawing him to FISHto's.

Sure, Michael Jordan the Goat was leading now, but

Sheed had the sense that even if MJ wasn't around, he would've found himself here eventually.

"You okay?" Otto watched him, always knew when something was off.

"I don't know. I'll probably have a better answer once we go in."

Michael Jordan the Goat stood at the entrance, waiting, his bag still dangling from his teeth, unable to operate the door handle.

Leen asked, "Does the goat walk up to the drive-thru to get his bag, or does someone come out here to give it to him?"

"Sis," said Wiki. "Bigger issues."

Someone did emerge from the back of the restaurant, opening the door for the goat, and the rest of them.

The man wore white shoes, and white pants, and a blue Monte FISHto's apron that was dusted with flour, and batter, and grease. His face was plump, clean-shaven, red at the cheeks and forehead. His woolly red hair stretched the limits of the hairnet he'd crammed it into. He waved his arm, welcoming. Michael Jordan the Goat clopped past him. The kids didn't move.

"Otto, Sheed, Wiki, and Leen! I'm so happy you made it. Come in," said the stranger.

Glances all around confirmed no one knew this guy. Otto understood they were hero-celebrities to the county

—maybe that was how he knew their names. This felt like a night for extra cautions, though.

"I don't mean to be rude, mister," Otto said, "but who are you?"

"I'm Stu. The cook. I've been expecting you."

Sheed said, "About that . . . how you been expecting us when nothing is going as expected tonight? Just seems" — he almost said *weird*, but the word tasted bad in his mouth now — "*suspicious*."

He didn't know if he'd ever said the word *suspicious* before. He checked with Otto for confirmation he'd used it right. Otto gave him a thumbs-up. Definitely suspicious.

Stu said, "I would tell you that you can trust me. An untrustworthy person would likely say the same, so that doesn't really help, does it?"

It didn't.

Stu motioned beyond them. "I don't think you'll want to stay outside with those folks, though. They look rather unpleasant."

The Money Zombie herd had turned the corner and was getting closer.

Wiki said, "Let's take our chances with Stu."

She and Leen ran inside FISHto's. After a second's hesitation, Otto and Sheed did too.

Stu closed and locked the door behind them. There was still a problem.

"This place is lit up like the Fifth of July," said Sheed.

Stu frowned. "Don't you mean the Fourth of July?"

Otto explained, "Not after last year. The Fourth was the county fireworks show. The Fifth was the time the spooky old Machen house became translucent with ectoplasmic energy. Way brighter than the fireworks."

"Oh." Stu nodded. "I do see your point. No worries. You're safe here in FISHto's."

"How?" said Wiki. She and Leen dragged a heavy table over to barricade the door. "FISHto's is still in Fry with *those things!*"

The Money Zombies reached the door, pounding on it and flattening their GOO, Inc., checks against the glass so the commas and zeroes were easily read.

Otto and Sheed grabbed a second table to block the entrance across the lobby that Money Zombies were rushing. After all they'd done to escape Mayor Ahmed's office, it looked like they'd traded one dead end for another.

Otto told Stu, "Maybe you can help us put something else heavy in front of the door."

"No need," Stu said. Michael Jordan the Goat rubbed his head against Stu's hip, and the man gently scratched between MJ's horns.

"As I said," Stu continued, "when you're here, you're safe because here can be anywhere there's a FISHto's. Watch."

The cook snapped his fingers. Michael Jordan the Goat *baaaed!* The Money Zombies vanished.

"No way!" Leen tugged her goggles over her eyes to take environmental readings, hoping some quick measurements of temperature and moisture in the air, or something in the ultraviolet light spectrum might explain what happened.

Wiki didn't need her sister's tech to understand what was wrong. She pointed at a window, beyond the glass. "That's not Fry."

Not only had the Money Zombies vanished, so had the familiar downtown buildings that should've surrounded the restaurant. Nobody recognized any of the structures filling the darkness around them now. No one but Stu. He said, "This is a town called Green Creek. FISHto's store number 6120."

Otto's stomach felt wishy-washy. He went for his Legendary Log and pencil for comfort.

Sheed was so over all the weird that he couldn't control his sudden outburst. "Tell us what's happening and stop being mysterious, dude!"

Stu flinched, snapped his fingers again, and suddenly the buildings outside weren't the kind found in small-town Virginia. They were clay colored, with a sheen of dust. Between them sand, rocks, and cacti—a desert at night.

"This is store number 3317," Stu said, "Las Vegas, Nevada."

Stu snapped his fingers again, and the world outside became bright sunshine with a great view of a pagoda. "Hanoi, Vietnam."

Again. "Sydney, Australia."

Again. "Accra, Ghana."

"You're teleporting us!" Wiki said, knees weak.

"In a sense."

"Could you please stop!"

Stu snapped his fingers once more, bringing them back to nighttime, though still not in Fry. "This is Portside, Virginia, store number 2115. We're closer to your home, but without all the extra company. So we can talk in peace."

Otto's neck craned, trying to understand. "What *is* this place?"

"It's the Count of Monte FISHto's. Home of the Cra-Burger. Or, as the jingle goes"—Stu's voice got singsongy—"*Surf and Land, all in one hand!*"

Late and tone-deaf, Leen came in on ". . . *all in one hand!*"

Wiki stared at her sister. Hard.

"What?" said Leen. "That jingle's a catchy song."

"How does it work?" Otto scribbled while he spoke. "Is the building moving, or just us?"

"It's only us. All the Monte FISHto's franchises reside on fixed points in space. Over ten thousand locations. Each built on very specific plots of land where certain energies are present. Those energies can be used by any high-ranking employee to make sure all the locations are serviced properly."

Sheed said, "Dude, what's that even mean?"

"Right now, because you're with me, you have the ability to be in any and every Monte FISHto's with a mere thought."

"And what are you again?" Wiki said.

"Stu. The cook."

Wiki smacked her forehead.

Leen pointed to Michael Jordan. "What about the goat?"

Stu said, "Oh, I really don't know. That's a Logan County thing, but he's been very helpful in leading you here."

Michael Jordan the Goat *baaaaaaed*.

Otto thought aloud, trying to work this mess out. "We first saw the goat when we went to Dr. Medina's. You knew we'd go there?"

"Yes."

Confusion was thick in the air.

Sheed, doing his very best not to explode, clenched his fists. "How and why?"

"I'm the Quest Giver, I know things. It was all so you could find your way to me and be prepared for the dangers ahead. It's part of the Quest Rules."

Otto, for once, was not the calm one. "That's dumb. You could've just told us. Like, hey, Legends, I'm Stu from the magical fish restaurant, and I have information you need. Doing it this way doesn't prepare us for jack. We are *unprepared!*"

Stu scoffed. "Since the beginning of time, Quest Givers

like myself have provided obscure and somewhat puzzling clues for heroes like you to follow."

Wiki said, "In the beginning of time, they didn't have email."

Stu frowned. "True. I didn't think of that. I did consider a lengthy text message, but in my research I couldn't find a cell number for either of you Legendary Alstons."

Sheed pointed at Otto. "Write that down for Grandma!"

"Quest Givers and Quest Rules, though?" Leen had removed her goggles and was cleaning the lenses with a FISHto's napkin. "Seems really inefficient, if you ask me. I have thoughts on how to improve your system."

"We can talk about reworking the Quest Rules system later," said Otto, "Do you want to get on with it, Stu? What's all this about?"

"It's about GOO, Inc. Or as they've been known throughout most of history, the Great Old Ones. It's time you learned what they are and what they plan to do. More importantly, why they cannot be allowed to succeed. All you know and love depends on it."

Leen clapped and laughed. Startling everyone.

"Sorry," she said, "I was still thinking about the jingle. *All in one hand!*"

23

Never Just Stories

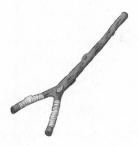

THE LEGENDARY ALSTON BOYS and the Epic Ellisons had a seat, while Michael Jordan the Goat brought each of them a bag of their favorite (or *most tolerable,* since the food here was mediocre at best) FISHto's menu item. Such a skilled goat.

Stu paced while he talked, looking like someone on a stage before hundreds instead of the four-person (and a goat) audience he actually had. Otto got the sense he'd been waiting a long time for this. "The creature that controls GOO, Inc., Nyarlathotep, is one of many ancient beings."

Otto spoke through a mouthful of Cra-Burger: "There are more of those three-headed snakes out there?"

Stu said, "They're all different. No less ugly, though. All have varying, usually chaotic, goals. No love for humanity whatsoever."

Otto took a lot of notes, but stopped to say, "Why does this sound familiar?"

Wiki answered. "H. P. Lovecraft, the old-school horror writer and horrible racist. His stories were about this kind of stuff."

"They weren't just stories," Stu said. "They're never just stories."

Wiki shuddered.

Leen said, "You okay, sis?"

"There's a downside to never being able to forget stuff. Stories like this are not very fun to remember. Super creepy."

Stu went on. "We—me and the folks behind Monte FISHto's—have fought the Great Old Ones forever. Sometimes we win, sometimes they do. Every decade or so we find ourselves tussling with the Great Old Ones. This time the fight is here in Logan County . . . when it's not supposed to be. Something new has drawn Nyarlathotep to battle way sooner than expected."

"U-rays," Otto said.

Stu eyed a scowling Sheed. "Is that what you're calling it?"

"That's what *he's* calling it," said Sheed.

"Whatever you call it, it's strong in you. I feel it. I can see why Nyarlathotep craves it. Based on that monster's latest scheme, it seems to have found the perfect way to tap into the modern world's most powerful weapon. Money."

Money. Money. Money. Is that what it
all comes back to with grownups? I
mean, I get you gotta pay for stuff
(sidenote: I'm hoping these FISHto's
meals are gifts because I don't have
any actual money with me now), but
if it makes you side with monsters—or
become the monsters like all the Money
Zombies back in Fry—how can it ever
be a good thing?

Deduction: I don't have a deduction
for this. I just don't know.

Wiki said, "So when the Great Old Ones formed a
company and started fighting for money, your side decided
the best way to challenge them was to open up a fish sandwich place?"

"First and foremost," Stu said, indignant, "Monte
FISHto's opened because our recipe is second to none. Our
rich buttermilk batter, with our secret seasoning mix . . .
There's a reason our sandwiches are ranked Top Nine—
sometimes Top Seventeen—in every country in the world."

Wiki wasn't impressed.

"Um, but yes," Stu said, "we make a lot of money with the recipe, and that allows us to combat GOO, Inc., on their terms. If they build a chemical plant that pollutes the atmosphere, we can build windmills to help cut pollution. If they burst an oil line and spill into the ocean, we can send vessels that aid the cleanup effort."

Leen said, "You're the good guys?"

Stu beamed.

But he did not answer, Otto noticed and noted.

"That sounds like a tug-of-war," Sheed said. "One nobody ever really wins."

"That may not be true this time," Stu said, grave. "This weirderfront property play of theirs may tip the scales. What they're buying from the residents of this county is going to be worth so much money over time. If they get their hands on a certain somebody who has the ability to draw weirdness to him, theoretically, they could create more weirderfront property wherever they want. GOO, Inc.'s funds —their power—would be *unlimited*."

Sheed said, "I'm really sick of bad guys liking me."

Otto felt Sheed's pain and was willing to let him sulk for a bit. In the meantime, they needed a plan. "You got us here. You told us what the Great Old Ones are. Now, what are we all going to do about it?"

"You have the Keys to the City, yes?"

Otto and Wiki nodded.

"Good. Now I must give you the riddle in which lies the answer to the location of the locks."

They groaned.

"Dude!" Sheed said.

"Could you please just tell us where the locks are?" said Otto.

"This is ridiculous," said Wiki.

Leen pouted. "I don't even want to sing your jingle now."

Stu held his hands out defensively, clearly sorry about the complicated nature of his role in this quest. "This is simply the way things are done."

"Quest Rules!" Sheed threw up his hands in resignation. "What's the dag-gone riddle, Stu?"

Stu cleared his throat and projected like a Shakespearean actor. "*Where it started is where it will end.*"

"Where what started?" said Wiki.

"'*It*.' Were you not listening?" Stu snapped his fingers. The scenery outside of Monte FISHto's changed again. Became familiar again.

They were back in Fry. No Money Zombies in sight.

Stu said, "Fortunately, your pursuers have short attention spans and have moved on. For now. If you move quickly and quietly, you may be able to solve the riddle without alerting them."

An exasperated Wiki said, "Or you could tell us the precise location of the locks."

Stu said, "No, but I'm more than happy to fill a to-go order so you don't get hungry. Michael Jordan!"

The goat perked up, but Otto waved off the offer. "No, let's get to it. Quests don't finish themselves."

They gathered their belongings and slid the table barricades aside, ready to leave. Otto asked, "If we find the locks, will we know what to do with whatever's on the other side?"

"You're smart children. I'm sure you'll have an inkling."

"Do you care about us saving Logan County, or just beating GOO, Inc.?"

Stu said, "Does it really matter in the end?"

Otto got mad at himself, because he didn't know how to answer *that* particular riddle either.

24

Under Locks and Keys

ENTRY #50

"Where it started is where it will end."

What. Does. That. Mean????

Maybe "it" is the Rorrim Mirror
Emporium, because that's what led to
Sheed getting V-rays?

Or, what if "it" is the frog storm that
brought Mom, Uncle Solo, and GOO,
Inc., to Fry? So, back at Grandma's
house?

Grrrrrr. "It" could literally be anything.

*Deduction: We should've let Leen
rework the quest system for maximum
efficiency!*

Otto pocketed his pad. "Y'all got anything?"

"I have a tummy ache from the Carp Nuggets," said Leen.

It was late, cold — they could see their breath — and the continuous breeze that began following them shortly after they left Monte FISHto's didn't do much to relieve their discomfort.

"What about you, Windy?" Otto asked. "You got anything?"

Windy blasted them with a couple of frosty gusts that Otto interpreted as *I got nothing, dawg.*

They'd gotten out of downtown. Maybe sticking to the edges of Fry would make it easier to avoid Money Zombies. While the plan seemed solid, Sheed voiced their biggest problem after a monster yawn. "I'm getting sleepy."

They all were.

Sheed rubbed his hands together to warm them. With the way the temperature was dropping, they wouldn't be able to stay outside for much longer. "If only Mayor Ahmed could've told us whatever he was going to say. Maybe the quest would be over by now."

"Instead we get an impossible riddle," Otto said. It did

look like the mayor was ready to give them a cheat code for this whole quest nonsense. If only . . .

Otto stopped walking. The crew and Windy continued on a few yards ahead before realizing they were missing someone.

"What?" Sheed said.

"Wiki," said Otto. "Were you watching Mayor Ahmed the whole time we were in his office?"

"Pretty much."

Wiki Ellison could memorize whole books by glancing at the pages. Replay movies in her head after seeing them once. And remember every little detail from their time in the mayor's office.

Otto said, "When he was talking about the location of the locks, what else was he doing?"

She squeezed her eyes shut. Whenever Otto saw her do this, he imagined a big screen on the back of her eyelids where she rewatched memories like an instant replay.

Wiki spoke as if she was back in the office, witnessing everything in real time. "He's super nervous. All kinds of tics from his face and hands. He walks over to the window, stares out. He's squinting and nodding. He's seeing something he wants to see and relaxes a little."

"Okay," Otto said. "Now, when you looked out the window, right before we jumped, what did *you* see?"

"Town Square. It's empty."

"When you look in the same direction Mayor Ahmed looked in when he got calm, does anything stand out?"

"Just the"—her eyes popped wide—"founder's statue."

"Where it all started is where it will end," Otto whispered.

"You're thinking Frederick Fryer put the locks in his father's statue? Because Fry started with him?"

"It's the best guess I've got."

Sheed felt a spike of anxiety over being closer to solving the riddle and defeating GOO, because it meant they were closer to waking up their parents and breaking up the family. He began to glow dully. "Well, let's go. Because I think my"—errrr, he hated saying it—*"U-rays* are acting up again."

They set a course back toward downtown, hoping to reach the statue before some other weird thing reached them first.

#

Fortunately, they made it back to Town Square without trouble. Unfortunately, what Otto hoped to find—five locks in plain sight, yay, quest complete—they didn't.

The statue of Fullerton French Fryer was twelve feet tall. Half of it was the man carved in stone, the other half was the boxy base he stood upon. Mounted to the four-sided pedestal were matching plaques (one on each side), describing some of the history Mayor Ahmed had covered. Schoolteacher. Schoolhouse. The town growing from there.

Otto said, "Leen, you seeing anything through your goggles?"

Leen's lenses whined, contracted, glowed red. "Looks like plain stone."

Otto got mad at himself for thinking it might be this easy. "Everyone take a side, look for anything—"

"Don't say 'weird,'" said Sheed.

"Unusual."

Sheed's glowing had subsided. Mostly. His slightly yellowish hue was still that of a drowsy firefly. Oh boy.

They searched, running fingers over the weather-stained plaques and rough concrete, looking for hidden hinges, or clasps, or compartments, or cubbies.

Over the engraved history on each plaque was an embossed image of Fullerton French Fryer's face. On Otto's side of the base, the image was slightly off center, as if Fullerton was tipping forward to bow. He ran his hand over the bronze face, worked his thumb and forefinger into the widest grooves, and turned.

Fullerton rotated so he was looking at the ground. "Hey, guys! Turn the faces clockwise."

He continued turning on his side, turning until Fullerton's nose was pointed toward the sky, and that was when a hidden clasp unlatched and the tiny image swung open on a hinge revealing a . . .

"Keyhole," Otto whispered.

Wiki was next. "Found it."

Then Leen. Then Sheed.

Four in all.

They pulled out their five keys—Otto taking great care to remove his from their decorative frames—fitting each to a particular lock through trial and error, eventually finding the perfect matches.

Otto circled the statue, wondering about the remaining key from Wiki and Leen's stash. Where was the fifth lock? "I guess we gotta turn these, see what happens."

Wiki said, "Seems like a good idea in theory, but we

still don't know what Stu or the mayor meant by unlocking the town's potential. What if its potential is a giant monster like in the Godzilla movies?"

Otto's first reaction was to dismiss such a silly notion. Then he remembered where they were . . . Nothing was ever really a silly notion in Logan County. Hello, ancient chaos gods and Money Zombies.

He said, "Turn the keys *slowly*, then."

They did, with only Sheed having to really put some muscle in it due to his lock being slightly rusty. When all four finished, a section of cement by Otto's feet groaned —the sound of old rock rubbing old rock. The ground sank in sections, forming a staircase that descended into shadow. Wiki, Leen, and Sheed crowded behind Otto.

Leen said, "Welp, guess we're going that way."

25

Support and Power

THE TUNNEL TOOK THEM DEEP beneath Town Square, making several sharp, odd turns before settling into the level floor of a vast cavern. The Legends and the Epics all carried flashlights, so the surrounding dark wasn't as intimidating as what the lights actually revealed: the entire underside of Fry stretching on and on well beyond their flashlight beams.

There were rusted steel columns supporting foundations. Thick pipes adorned with emblems for the electric and phone companies housing all the cables that kept the town powered up and its residents just a call away. Annnnd . . . a terrifying amount of goo!

Not the company Otto's mom worked for. Goo! Actual snotlike slime. The color of spinach. Slick and oozing around a number of the columns holding the town up.

Sheed said, "Oh, that's nasty."

Otto approached the nearest column caked in the stuff. "What is this?"

"Don't get too close," Wiki said. "I've seen a lot of movies, and you don't want to be in snatching distance of any mysterious slime."

Leen popped her goggles on and scanned a chunk of gunk. "Wik, you know where we are?"

"Yep, under City Hall. Facing south."

The twists and turns of the staircase had disoriented Otto and Sheed; they would've needed a compass to gauge where they were or what direction they were going in. The power of Wiki's memory made her a sort of human compass.

Otto turned, pointed in the opposite direction. "So Main Street's that way."

He shone his flashlight on more columns encased in gunk and delved into the dark. Sheed stuck with him. "What are you thinking, cuzzo?"

"Just a hunch. Wiki, do you know exactly what we're under here?"

"Nice Dream Ice Cream," she said.

"Naw," Sheed corrected. "It's Riches Brew now."

Whatever it was, the supports and cables dedicated to this particular business were heavily coated in the snot-slime.

Otto slashed his flashlight beam at a different column,

and the associated power and telephone cables. "What about that one? Is that Mr. Archie's hardware store?"

"Yeah," Wiki said, "it is. How'd *you* know?"

"Because it's not covered in goo." The supports and cables were dry, caked in old dust. Unbothered and unchanged. "He hasn't sold out to the company. Yet."

The four of them swept their flashlights around a whole underworld they never knew about. Which didn't offer an easy answer to Sheed's next question. "Which way do we go?"

They returned to the stairs that led them there. Tried to reason it out.

Otto said, "We're supposed to go where it all began, right?"

"That's what the magic guy who cooks fish patties said." Wiki did not sound convinced.

Sheed said, "Okay, let's brainstorm this thing. If—"

"It's that way." Leen pointed south.

Their flashlight beams fixed on her.

Wiki said, "How the heck do you know that?"

The owl lenses on her goggles contracted to red pinpoints. "Because I can see a weird, out-of-place door about a thousand yards ahead. Since we still have one key left— I mean, I think this is the Quest Rules being literal. The town's potential is probably behind that door."

Glances all around. Wiki said, "The logic seems sound to me."

They went that way.

The nearly mile-long trek toward the door generated a mix of pride and revulsion in Otto. The slimy, goo-covered landmarks around them were plenty gross, and he couldn't imagine any amount of money making him okay with this kind of corruption happening right beneath his feet. The pride came in recognizing the GOO, Inc., buyouts weren't as widespread as he thought. The amount of *uncorrupted* support and power beneath their home reminded Otto that a lot of the county folk were still resisting the GOO, Inc., influence. As Grandma would say, those folks *ain't fall for the okey-doke.*

ENTRY #51

When it comes to the properties over our heads, the logic seems consistent. The ones that have been sold to the evil company have all their support and connections looking like wet boogers. When someone gives up a piece of the town to the GOO, it changes everything. The stuff you can see and the stuff you can't.

Deduction: Not everyone in our community can be bought, though. That *might help us in the fight to keep it "our" community. Maybe.*

That deduction left Otto troubled. Sure, they could fight Goo, Inc. Of course! Him and Sheed and Wiki and Leen had been in spectacular battles before. But when it came to the power of money . . . how could regular, everyday county folks win?

They reached the door. It was set in a chunk of solid stone, and didn't look strong. The vertical slats were loosely fastened to one another, flaking with dry rot in some places. Seemed like if you threw a rock hard enough, it would punch right through. Looks can be deceiving.

Otto pressed his palm against the weak-looking wood. It felt as solid as brick. Sheed tugged the knob, putting all his strength into it. It didn't give. Wiki crouched and peeked through a gap in the boards: darkness beyond.

Otto said, "Where are we, Wiki? What are we under?"

"Right now? A field, by the . . . Wait a minute."

The fifth key—the only one they hadn't used yet—was still on a length of chain around Wiki's neck. She tugged it over her head and stuck it into the lock. A smooth fit. She turned it, then tugged the door open. Another staircase. She darted up.

"Wik!" Leen said, chasing.

Sheed went after her. Otto didn't love the idea of rushing blindly up into the town's "potential"—what if it was, like, a secret nuclear reactor or something?—but he wasn't about to let his friends go it alone.

The stairs were numerous, and twisting, and Otto felt that same sense of disorientation he'd felt descending beneath the town at the founder's statue. The higher he got, the less he relied on his flashlight as some other source of illumination dissolved the gloom. He still heard the clopping footfalls of everyone else ahead of him. Then the sound of squeaky door hinges, and Wiki's voice, faint but clear —and annoyed—echoing toward him.

"Seriously?" she said.

The floor leveled, there were long fluorescent bulbs in ceiling panels above his head, and when he stepped through the open door that Sheed, Leen, and Wiki crowded around, he understood Wiki's irritation.

There were in the hallway at D. Franklin Middle School.

Sheed said, "Quest Rules are sooooo stupid."

26

Locker Gnomes Are a Thing, Y'all!

OTTO, AS ANNOYED AS THE REST of them, said, "*We're* the potential?"

This reminded him of one of Grandma's records by the pretty lady with the pretty voice who sang about believing the children were the future, and that was cool and everything, but he couldn't really see how that was going to help them beat the three-headed snake god that was flooding the caverns beneath the town with money snot.

Leen said, "Guys. We're in the school after hours. Do you think there are any good leftovers in the cafeteria?"

Wiki said, "There would probably need to be good food before there are good leftovers, and that's never been the case. So, no."

Sheed said, "What now?"

He'd been on enough adventures and cases to know they were getting toward the end. After this mess was over, him and his dad would leave. Otto and Grandma would go with Aunt Cinda and Uncle DeMarcus. They'd be Legends no more.

In the half-lit hallway, Sheed's yellow aura pulsed in time with his heartbeat.

Leen said, "Are you okay? You're flashing."

He sulked. "I know. I'm trying to make it stop."

Sheed's glow was clearly visible and clearly disturbing *something* in the walls. They all heard scratching.

"Wait a second!" Otto said, aggravated, but not at Sheed. Time to test a theory. "Are you feeling really relaxed right now?"

"Why on earth would I feel relaxed right now?" The aura grew brighter.

Wiki and Leen tensed. The weird sounds weren't in the walls, but in the lockers. Louder now.

"Take a deep breath," Otto said.

Sheed did, though he looked extremely irritated.

"Now let it out."

He blew directly into Otto's face.

"That's just rude. Do you feel relaxed now?"

"No!" Sheed's aura flared bright.

Otto crept toward his own locker, spotting what seemed to be tiny eyes peering through the ventilation slits in the door.

"Do you feel relaxed now?" As he asked, he spun his locker's combination dial.

"No, stop asking me!" Sheed roared, glowing as bright and steady as sunshine.

Otto yanked his door open, exposing a plump, darkly clothed creature the approximate size of a mouse, with a face best described as half human, half beaver, with a stupid pointy hat on its head. It was perched on his locker shelf with a Bic pen in one hand and a half-worn eraser in another.

"I knew it!" Otto snatched the creature into the open for everyone to see. "Locker gnomes!"

"What the heck?" Leen shuffled backwards.

The gnome kicked and snarled in Otto's grasp.

Wiki said, "Of all the weirdness tonight, didn't see this coming. Care to explain, Otto?"

"You ever put something in your locker, like a pencil, or a paper clip? But when you go to your locker to get it, you can't find it?" He held his captive at arm's length. "Locker gnomes! Cousins to sock gnomes, the ones who make sure you can never find a matching sock. Little thieves. You took my highlighter, didn't you?"

The creature snapped its jaws, though not in any real attempt to bite Otto. It was just so tiny and ornery.

Wiki and Leen trotted to their lockers, though Sheed remained still, frowning. Maybe he saw where Otto was going with this.

The girls found gnomes in their lockers, still and staring.

Otto would've bet there was a gnome in every locker. All in range of Sheed's energy, and all stuck in place.

Otto said, "There are two times I've noticed your U-rays really ramping up. When you're super relaxed, like when you're asleep. Those are the big steady pulses weird things feel all around the world. Then, when you're worked up about something, like now. What are you worked up about?"

Sheed didn't like Otto analyzing him, and certainly didn't want to fess up to being scared about their parents splitting the family up soon. He stepped past Otto and felt several dozen gnome eyes following him behind locker vents.

Otto knew Sheed didn't want to talk about what was

on his mind. Maybe because the girls were here, or maybe because he was very sensitive about it, and that made it hard to talk, no matter who was around.

Sheed didn't have to talk for Otto to test the next part of his theory. He was thinking of how Windy flinched when Sheed got mad back in Mr. Rickard's classroom, or how the animals at Dr. Medina's had started making noise when Sheed said he wished they would.

"Sheed," said Otto, "tell the locker gnomes they're free to go."

"Huh?"

"Just do it!"

Sheed huffed. "Go home, gnome guys."

The gnomes in Wiki's and Leen's lockers vanished into the shadows, presumably through some secret passage in the wall. The various eyes in the other lockers disappeared. The only gnome that remained was in Otto's hand, staring flatly at its captor.

Otto said, "Fine. You can go too."

It waved Otto's pen and eraser, the gesture an unspoken question Otto understood immediately.

"Yes, you can keep them."

The gnome smiled, nodded courteously. Otto placed it back on his locker shelf, allowing it to slink into the shadows.

"What was that?" Sheed said, confused but calming. His glow fading.

"Dude, not only do your U-rays draw weird things to you, I think they let you have some small influence over those weird things. You're like . . . *the Weird King!*"

Sheed liked that even less than the term *U-rays* and did not want to dwell on the awful title. "Tell me that's not what we came here for? For you to come up with that 'Weird King' mess!"

Leen said, "I think the Weird King's cool. Reminds me of something from *The Monarch's Gambit.*"

She flashed Sheed a smile, and suddenly he was no longer worried about U-rays, Otto's dumb name, or *Monarch's Gambit* spoilers.

"Okay, okay." Otto used his voice of reason. "Back to the quest. Maybe there's something here we can use to do something with our potential, I guess?"

They fanned out. Checked classrooms and supply closets, almost wishing there was another riddle that might help them decipher how their "potential" was supposed to help the town in the current crisis.

Otto's piece of the search brought him closer to the auditorium. Light applause cheered him on. He grinned, happy for the encouragement. Until he realized no one should be applauding at the school in the middle of the night.

"Hey," Otto called to the rest, motioning toward the sounds.

They tiptoed that way. The clapping had tapered off, replaced by lilting musical notes. Sheed looked to Otto, who only shook his head. He didn't know what was going on either.

At the auditorium entrance the four of them stacked up, nudged their heads between the double doors, and saw . . .

Juggling?

Onstage, with a spotlight illuminating her gray uniform and orange safety vest, was Ms. Carmichael, the school bus driver. She tossed five balls between her hands, with at least three of them airborne at all times.

Her audience: about a dozen of their classmates filling the middle sections of the two rows closest to the stage.

Leen said, "Is this a GOO thing?"

"I don't think so," Wiki said.

Otto and Sheed agreed. GOO things were scary. This was actually the first bit of fun any of them had had all day.

They stepped into the auditorium, made their way down the long aisle toward the stage. The kids in the seats twisted around, noticing them. Ms. Carmichael ceased her routine, snatching the flying balls from the air, then shielding her eyes from the spotlight for a better look. "Who's there?"

Madison Baptiste said, "It's the Alstons and the Ellisons. Things must be really bad."

"Whatever, Madison!" said Bryan Donovan. "If they're here, we're good. They fix stuff like this all the time."

"What's going on?" Sheed asked.

Ms. Carmichael took the short staircase off the stage to

greet them, smiling a strained smile. "Hey there, children. You're here *for the sleepover?*"

Otto said, "Sleepover?"

"We know there's no sleepover, Ms. Carmichael," said Madison. "We know this is the Apocalypse."

Overly cheery, her smile twitching, Ms. Carmichael said, "This is not the Apocalypse, Madison." The bus driver leaned closer to Otto, Sheed, Wiki, and Leen, whispered, "Is it?"

Wiki said, "This is not the Apocalypse." She waved at the stage. "What is *this*, though?"

Ms. Carmichael leaned in closer, whispered lower. "After the school closed, I went to drive all the kids on my route home. Some I dropped off seemed fine. Some"—she jerked her head toward the kids in the seats—"couldn't get into their houses. Their keys didn't work, and there were big SOLD signs in their yard. I didn't want to leave them, so they got back on my bus, and we drove around. Later, I saw some of their parents tackling other people around town and shoving little slips of paper in their hands—"

"Checks," Leen said, feeling she now had a good grasp on that part of how money worked.

"Well, whatever it was, they started acting weird, and I have an intuition, y'all. I can sense danger. Call it my 'Driver-Sense,' and it was *tingling!* Then I started hearing Mayor Ahmed over the bus radio saying folks needed to stay inside. I didn't have anywhere else to take my riders, so I brought them back to the school."

Bryan yelled, "We did karaoke for, like, two hours. Ms. Carmichael has a great voice."

"As do you, Bryan." Ms. Carmichael turned her attention back to the Legends and the Epics. "I'm so tired, and this school has *no coffee*. Not even in the teacher's lounge."

Sheed patted her on the shoulder. "Sit down for a while, Ms. Carmichael. We'll take it from here."

The woman collapsed into the nearest seat, her juggling balls falling from her pockets and rolling every which way.

Otto said, "What are we doing?"

Sheed threw his hands up and walked toward the stage. "I'm going to tell everyone what's really happening. That it's not the Apocalypse. Even if it don't feel much better than the Apocalypse."

Sheed took center stage. Otto decided he wasn't going to let Sheed explain it all alone—plus, his notes might come in handy. He joined his cousin at the microphone, swatted it twice—*THUMP-THUMP*—to make sure it was on, then let Sheed have the first word.

He said, "Show of hands, how many of y'all know about money and corporations?"

No hands raised. All blank stares.

Bryan told Madison, "Okay. Maybe it's the Apocalypse."

27

Like Bear Traps ... but Bees

WIKI AND LEEN FOUND A WHITEBOARD on wheels backstage. They brought it out and helped Otto draw charts and stuff while Sheed explained the whole GOO, Inc., wanting to buy up all the weirderfront property in Logan thing. It was a comprehensive lesson, on par with what a sane Mr. Rickard was known for in his popular and informative science class.

When Sheed finished, there were still blank stares.

"Any questions?" he said.

Everyone's hand went up. Even Ms. Carmichael's.

"Oookayyyy," Otto said. He pointed at Madison.

She stood, blushing. "This is more of a comment than a question, but this sounds like we're in big trouble. Good presentation, though." She sat down.

Sheed said, "*Questions?*"

Otto called on Ms. Carmichael.

"Yes, my name is Gabby Carmichael, and I'm very happy to be here. I have a two-part question. Do all of those GOO, Inc., workers really have the power to make any kind of deal on behalf of the company?"

Otto checked the notes he took on the email Nyarlathotep sent to the company. "I think so."

"Okay. Got it. The second part of my question is what if they made a deal to get a bunch of beehives, and then they put those beehives all around town for unsuspecting people to stumble upon? Like bear traps . . . but bees."

Awkward silence followed.

Finally, Leen said, "Lady, how tired are you?"

Ms. Carmichael opened her mouth to answer.

Sheed leaned into the mike before she could. "Beehive traps would be very bad. We'll just have to hope they don't think of that. Next question."

Wiki picked someone. They asked what they asked. But Otto's mind was elsewhere. On Ms. Carmichael's question.

What if they made a deal to get a bunch of beehives, and then they put those beehives all around town for unsuspecting people to stumble upon?

Well, not that part. That part was insane. The first part . . .

Do all of those GOO, Inc., workers really have the power to make any kind of deal on behalf of the company?

Otto had told the room that he thought that was the case. He kept rereading what he'd written in his Legend

Log about his mom's email. He'd jotted it down after they left Grandma's, so maybe it wasn't word-for-word. He needed to know *exactly* what that email said. He knew who *could* tell him.

"Wiki." He tugged her to the side of the stage, "Do you remember that email my mom got before we went on the run?"

Wiki's face was emotionless.

"Of course you do. Could you recite it for me, please?"

She didn't even hesitate. "*Dear loyal employees, we got called back to the home office unexpectedly, but will be returning to the Logan County project by private plane posthaste. In the meantime, we'd like to extend our vast purchasing and deal-making powers to all of you who are still on-site. Please, make any and every effort to—*"

"Stop!" Otto shouted. He ran to Sheed.

Sheed was in the middle of an answer. "—I *don't* think Komodo dragons are actually tiny dragons that lost their wings. Otto, what are you doing?"

Otto dragged him from the mike. "We gotta go."

"Where?"

"To get our parents. We need them. Now!"

Sheed snatched away from Otto. "Explain."

"On the way. Ms. Carmichael?"

She'd nodded off, snoring softly. At the sound of her name, she jerked awake. "Oh, hey there."

"Can you drive us somewhere? Fast?"

"I could, the bus is outside, but—" She motioned to the kids in the seats. "I ain't leaving them."

"They can come," Otto said. "We're just going to Mr. Rickard's house."

Sheed growled. "*Explain.*"

And now everyone was listening.

Otto's brain was racing. Best-case scenarios. Worst-case scenarios. His overactive mind formulating the plan and trying to poke holes in it at the same time because there could not be any mistakes here. This was their last chance to save Logan County. And themselves.

Otto hadn't worked it all the way out, so he was hesitant to say too much. What he did say: "We're going to make the deal of a lifetime!"

\#

Everyone filed toward the bus in a heavy, and welcome, draft.

"Windy!" Leen yelled into the sky.

The elemental peeked over the edge of the school roof, bashful.

While Ms. Carmichael got most of the kids onto the bus, Otto spoke to Sheed and the Ellisons.

"Wiki, Leen—I got a job for you."

"We're listening," said Wiki.

"I need you two to go back to Monte FISHto's and—" Otto explained as much as he could as quickly as he could, because who knew how much time they had? A horde of

Money Zombies could be on them at any moment. Or, worse, Nyarlathotep could return from New York, and no telling what would happen then.

He finished describing the plan. Leen calibrated her gauntlet and goggles with a series of quick button pushes. "We can definitely do that."

"We can do much more," Wiki said. "But we'll take this menial task for the sake of time and efficiency. Let's go, Leen."

"Bye, Sheed," Leen said in her airy we-all-know-you're-my-boyfriend voice.

"Bye, Leen," Sheed said in the exact same way.

Otto pretended to vomit.

Wiki swatted him on the back of the head.

"Hey!" Otto shouted, afraid.

"Are you ever going to grow up?" Wiki said. "Let's go, Leen."

"Okay, okay," Leen said. "Just don't hit me, too." She called over her shoulder, "Windy, come watch our backs."

The Ellisons ran into the night with the howling elemental in tow.

Otto stood there, rubbing the stinging spot on the back of his head. "What's up with her?"

Sheed smirked. "Somehow, I don't think you're going to need my help to deduce that one. Come on, cuzzo. Let's go save stuff."

28

Bombs Away

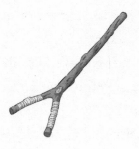

OTTO, SHEED, MS. CARMICHAEL, and twelve of D. Franklin Middle School's shining students bounced in their school bus seats on the way to Mr. Rickard's. They'd been on guard, expecting a Money Zombie attack—or, at the very least, a roadblock requiring a detour. Thankfully, the trip there was largely uneventful. (The one mild event being an intense thumb wrestling battle between Madison and Bryan—Madison won.)

Ms. Carmichael parked on the quiet street. She flipped the lever that folded the school bus door open. Otto and Sheed poked their heads out, searching one direction, then another. Nothing.

The boys hopped off, uncomfortable with how comfortably everything was going. Yet, they could not stop.

Otto told Ms. Carmichael, "We're going in to wake up our parents."

"Ten-four, Captain."

The overly formal response was unexpected, but . . . okay.

The boys ran across the lawn, Sheed's stomach twisting because he was pretty sure he'd be getting yelled at by a bunch of grownups shortly.

As if he didn't know about his role in the plan, Otto, being Otto, reminded Sheed. Again. "If we're lucky, they'll be waking up already. If we're not, you made the wish, so you might have to say it."

Sheed shouldered open Mr. Rickard's front door. "I got this."

Did he, though?

Otto's first and immediate fear—that their parents wouldn't be there, or that something horrible had happened to them while they were defenseless—was relieved. His mom, Uncle Solo, Grandma, and Bernard the monkey were right where they'd left them, sleeping peacefully. Bernard sucked his only thumb like a baby.

"Great," Otto said, consulting his notes. "Not exactly what I wanted. I'd hoped that since you wished they'd sleep until we needed them and now we actually need them, they'd already be awake. But we can work with this. You made the wish, so it's not an unreasonable assumption that you simply *saying* we need them will do the trick."

Sheed stared at his dad, who was flopped on his back, grinning, looking carefree.

Otto nudged his shoulder. "Soooo, say it."

Solo giggled, amused by something in a good dream. It irked Sheed. His dad always seemed most happy when he was alone and unbothered by anyone else.

"Sheed!" Otto said.

Sheed said, "Fine. You. Are. Needed. Wake up."

Cinda shifted and fell off the couch with a thud. Otto ran to her. "Mom!"

She wasn't hurt. Also, she wasn't awake. Otto shook her. "Mom."

Sheed picked his 'fro nervously.

No one was waking up. Otto remembered what Wiki said earlier. *What if you never think you need them?*

"Sheed, try again."

He said, "Everyone, we need you. Wake up." He sounded slightly more convincing that time. Not convincing enough.

Otto leapt over the coffee table and grabbed Bernard's wrist, yanking his thumb from his mouth. "I wish everyone in this room was awake."

Nothing happened.

Otto waved Bernard's arm toward Sheed. "You try."

Sheed grabbed the monkey's wrist, repeated Otto's wish. Still nothing.

Otto said, "He probably needs to be awake for it to work. Shoot."

"I'm sorry," Sheed said. "I messed this up bad, huh?"

"We don't have time for blame now. We'll solve this.

Just not here. Go grab some people off the bus. We'll need help carrying them."

"We're going to take them with us?"

"The bus is safe. Shouldn't be an issue at all." Otto immediately regretted saying it. Because Logan County listens. And laughs.

#

The D. Franklin Middle School classmates were more than happy to help, and with everyone chipping in, getting the adults from Mr. Rickard's house to the bus was a fairly easy task. The hardest part was transporting Grandma's and Cinda's big heavy purses—each required their carriers to take a brief break in Mr. Rickard's front yard.

"What's in this thing?" Bryan said, gasping, nearly lowering Grandma's bag onto the lawn.

Madison, who'd slung Cinda's purse over her shoulder, trudged past him like she was dragging a boulder and said, "None of your business, and you better not let it touch the ground. Black ladies don't play about their purses."

Bryan straightened up and struggled on.

Otto had his mom by her shoulders, while the middle school's best athlete, Cam Connor, held her legs. They carried her onto the vehicle while Ms. Carmichael motioned to a seat mid-bus. "I got a spot for her right here."

Otto and Cam got Cinda resting at her designated space, a seat next to a snoring Solo, across from a whinnying Grandma, and diagonal from a gassy Bernard (no one was happy about that, but Madison just opened several windows).

Sheed paced the aisle, trying to figure how he might undo what he'd done. They didn't really know how the wishes worked, and Bernard told them the wishes could go bad. Maybe it wouldn't do anything if he managed to really, sincerely feel like he needed his dad. Maybe that wasn't the key at all.

He pulled himself from his troubled thoughts to find Otto staring a hole in him. His cousin mouthed, *NEED. YOUR. DAD. NOW.*

"I'm trying."

As far back as he could remember, Sheed had convinced himself he didn't need anyone but Otto and Grandma. He knew they needed him. That was always enough because it had to be. Now he was supposed to make himself need the guy who sometimes forgot his birthday? The guy who went off to grieve all by himself for someone they both lost?

Otto came to him, placed his hands on Sheed's shoulders. "Grandma says when you stress yourself about stuff, it makes it harder to do stuff. Let's drive to FISHto's, you try to relax, and when we connect with Wiki, Leen, and Stu, we'll fix everything."

Sheed barely heard the last part, the roaring jet engine overhead was a little too loud.

"Cuzzo—"

Otto and Sheed stepped off the bus, looked up. As did Ms. Carmichael and the other D. Franklin Middle School students.

Way overhead, they saw the flashing wing lights of a low-flying jet. There was no doubt whose jet it was. Nyarlathotep had returned.

"They still have to land," Otto said, "then drive here. We've got time."

The roaring engine was joined by a shrill whistling. They'd heard the noise before. In war movies, when bombs fall.

"Let's get on the bus," Ms. Carmichael said. When no one moved, her voice shifted to the rough bark of a drill sergeant's. "ON THE BUS!"

The scramble was real. The kids piled on, with Otto and Sheed urging them along.

That whistling sound became piercing, and the boys spotted a dark bloated shadow that was a stain on the starless night sky. Falling, seemingly growing larger with every second it dropped.

Otto said, "No . . ."

"Way," said Sheed.

The writhing mass hit Mr. Rickard's roof with a fantastic *BOOM!* caving in the whole structure, exploding the windows, and collapsing the walls—leaving the whole thing a pile of rubble. The debris shifted and opened like

a mouth, which the creature Nyarlathotep slithered from python-quick. It brushed wood, plaster, and concrete from its black blazers and turtleneck sweaters.

Shaking off a cloud of dust, the creature pinned the boys with all six of its eyes.

"Now, that was . . ."

"Unpleasant, but we'll . . ."

"Be sure to . . ."

"Share all . . ."

"Our pain . . .

"And discomfort."

29

They Fly Now

OTTO AND SHEED RAN INSIDE THE BUS. Sheed flipped the lever that sealed the door.

"Ms. Carmichael," Otto said, "Let's go."

She twisted the key in the ignition. Then twisted it again. The engine *chuff-chuffed-chuffed* like it had a cold and was trying to cough up phlegm.

Ms. Carmichael said, "It stalls sometimes."

Awesome.

Half the kids pressed their faces to the windows closest to Nyarlathotep. The other half looked toward the two emergency exits—one at the back of the bus, the other a hatch in the roof. Except those weren't going to be of much use. More engines revved in the night.

Three of the GOO, Inc., tanker trucks crested the hill, riding toward them. Followed by slow hordes of Money Zombies led by the hazard-suited GOO, Inc., workers.

Nyarlathotep's faces grinned.

Ms. Nyar, voice booming loud enough to be heard over, well, everything, said, "Listen up. Here's what we're going to do, children. Most of you will come work for us. Great . . ."

"Wages, incredible benefits," Ms. Latho continued. "Just no free will. Trust us, it's a good trade. It's a good trade . . ."

"*For us.* But, for the Alstons and that monkey who humiliated us—we have such delicious terrors planned for them," said Ms. Tep.

Otto's jaw tightened. Sheed sneered.

"Not you, Rasheed. With your ability to draw weirdness to you, we're going to . . ."

"Take you to every little burg across the nation, creating our own weirderfront . . ."

"Property and becoming rich beyond rich until nothing in this world can stop us."

An angry Sheed flipped the lever, opening the school bus door so they got every single word of his response. "I ain't going anywhere with you, monster. Or *monsters.* I don't know if the three-heads thing means you're plural. But, whatever, that goes for all of you."

Ms. Nyar said, "Oh, child, you're as clueless as Don Glö from *The Monarch's Gambit* . . ."

Ms. Latho said, "When he learned that he could telepathically control the Falcon Steads, but . . ."

Ms. Tep said, "That same power was destined to corrupt him to the dark side."

Otto's and Sheed's hearts skipped several beats.

"Wait," Otto said, his fury rising in a way he was unaccustomed to. "Did you just reveal *The Monarch's Gambit* plot twist?"

Sheed said, "We made it through the entire day without knowing. You didn't even say 'spoiler alert.' You truly are evil."

Otto snapped, threw himself toward the open door. Sheed hooked an arm around Otto's waist before he went too ballistic.

Otto said, "Let me at them, Sheed. They've got to pay."

"When did you get so strong?" Sheed strained to keep his cousin from busting loose. Then, to Ms. Carmichael, "How we coming on getting the bus started, ma'am?"

"I'm sweet-talking her." Ms. Carmichael twisted the ignition and massaged the dashboard. "My M1 Abrams used to be temperamental like this. Give her a second."

Sheed had a moment to think, *Isn't an M1 Abrams a tank?*

Then things outside changed in a more *disturbing* way. The expressionless Money Zombies flanked Nyarlathotep. Several GOO, Inc., employees in bright yellow hazard suits formed a line in front of the boss monster.

"Now, we think . . ."

"It's time for . . ."

"Some company expansions."

The workers in the yellow hazard suits began to twitch

and shake like bad dancers. Their suits bulged at the hands, feet, and back. Talons erupted through their boots. Claws unsheathed from their gloved fingertips. At the point where their backs met their shoulders, wings composed of long bones and veiny flesh, like those of a bat, erupted into the open, flexing and flapping.

"Uh-oh," said Sheed.

Otto got much less anxious to be outside the bus. "Those guys fly now?"

A massive shudder shook the bus. Ms. Carmichael finally coaxed the engine to life. "Hang on, everyone!"

Otto flipped the lever, resealing the door.

Ms. Carmichael stomped the gas pedal, rocketing the bus forward, and Nyarlathotep's troops charged.

The road ahead was blocked by Money Zombies, and Otto feared Ms. Carmichael would plow right through them, but she spun her big steering wheel left and took the bus off-road. Or, rather, on-yard, cutting through a grassy lawn, knocking aside plastic pink flamingos and plaster lawn jockeys.

"Where to?" Ms. Carmichael said.

Otto held on to the closest seat with one hand and pointed with the other. "There."

The tall and glowing Monte FISHto's sign shined in the night sky, approximately four miles away.

Ms. Carmichael nodded. Then glanced in her rearview mirror, her face tightening. "We got a tail."

Sheed ran down the aisle to the back of the bus, trying not to meet the terrified glances of his schoolmates, and saw what looked like all of GOO, Inc., in pursuit. The (now-flying) hazard-suited employees, the Money Zombies (though, thankfully, they were falling behind . . . not fast enough to keep up).

The GOO, Inc., tanker trucks were another story. They were gaining, and for some reason, several bat-winged employees affixed themselves to the sides of the tankers and uncoiled the vacuum hoses. Then there was the boss monster, Nyarlathotep, giving chase in a series of slithering leaps that were a horror to watch. No natural creature moved like that.

Ms. Carmichael burst through a backyard fence, splintering the wood and sending the kids at the back of the bus bouncing toward the ceiling. Someone shouted, "Wheee!" before remembering this wasn't a joyride.

Among those bouncing bodies, Otto's mom, Sheed's dad, Grandma, and Bernard. Going airborne and never losing a bit of the supernatural slumber that gripped them as they fell back into their designated seats.

Sheed knew it—*felt* it. He *needed to need* his father. He needed to wake them all up, because the truth was Ms. Carmichael, as skilled as she was at handling the cumbersome bus, wasn't going to beat all of these foes to FISHto's. Not on her own. Even if she did, if the adults were still asleep, Otto's plan wouldn't work. The trip would be for nothing.

Otto was occupied at the front of the bus helping Ms. Carmichael navigate. The rest of the kids gripped their seats for dear life. Sheed slipped onto the seat where his dad was curled up like a baby, snoring, and whispered in his ear. "It's hard to be with you sometimes because I don't think I really know you, or that you really know me. But if you ever wanted to make things right between us, I *need you to wake up right now!*"

Solo's eyes popped open like window shades. He sat up quick, yawning and stretching. In the next seat Cinda emerged rubbing grit from her eye. Grandma sat up, grinding a fist into her lower back and muttering, "Ooooh, chile. I'mma need some IcyHot."

Bernard hopped onto his hind legs and monkey screeched, and several children screamed in response.

Otto spun around, went bug-eyed when he saw his mother squinting, fluffing out her bed hair, and looking around all confused.

"Mom!" He ran down the aisle and hopped into her arms.

Cinda kissed Otto's forehead while glancing around. "We're on a bus."

Solo blinked rapidly and clasped a hand on Sheed's shoulder. "Hey, bud . . . you got a situation report for us?"

Sheed pointed to the back, beyond the window. "Aunt Cinda's bosses wanna talk."

The adults and Bernard looked that way, their groggy faces turned alert and grim.

Bernard raised his paw, with two of the fingers curled inward, while the rest remained straight and unused. "I have some wishes left in me before I need time to reset. I can attempt to wish Nyarlathotep away again—"

"No!" Otto broke free of his mom's embrace and hopped the seat to join the monkey. "We want it to follow us so we can end this once and for all. We need to get to where we're going, though."

"Where's that?" Cinda asked.

"Monte FISHto's."

Grandma said, "I ain't even going to ask."

Bernard said, "Very well. Perhaps I can thin the herd with some wishes. That will help ease the—"

The window nearest Bernard exploded inward, and one of the flying GOO, Inc., employees snatched the monkey away, his monkey shrieks fading as he disappeared into the night.

A moment of stunned silence stretched.

Sheed said, "Y'all might want to get away from the windows."

Everyone slid closer to the center of the bus.

If losing Bernard wasn't bad enough, a familiar and unsettling sound echoed inside the rolling yellow tin can. *THUMP. TH-THUMP-THUMP.*

Behind them, the flying employees kept pace with the

tanker trucks, bouncing in the air while aiming the vacuum hoses at the bus, the same vacuum hoses they'd used to suck up the Tooth Frogs after the storm at Grandma's. They'd reversed the switches, turning the sucking air into blowing air. The hoses became cannons, shooting Tooth Frogs at the bus in bursts.

The fat amphibians sailed through the air, smacking the bus, sticking to roof, sides, and back like boogers. Where they landed, they gnawed, grinding their needle teeth against metal and glass.

By Otto's estimation, they still had three long, bumpy

miles to go. Too far for the bus not to get overwhelmed and shredded. If those things got to the tires . . . or inside to their classmates!

"Alstons," Otto shouted, "time for a family meeting."

For once, no one argued.

30

Spoiler Alert

OTTO SPOKE FAST. "WE GOTTA KEEP this bus moving, no matter what. Ms. Carmichael can handle the driving—"

Ms. Carmichael shouted from the front, "You got that right! This is just like my time in the war."

"What war?" Sheed said under his breath.

Otto continued, "It's up to us to keep as many of these frogs off the bus as we can. What weapons do we have?"

He dug in his backpack while Mom and Grandma went for their purses. Solo checked his coat pockets while Sheed produced several spare Afro picks from, apparently . . . *the depths of his hair?*

Between them they had two collapsible batons, brass knuckles, a Warped World slingshot Otto loved with his whole heart, Solo's half-empty bottle of cologne that also doubled as pepper spray, and a fidget spinner.

"It'll have to do," Otto said.

Sheed said, "What's the plan, cuzzo?"

Otto motioned to the exit hatch in the ceiling. "We go up, keep the Tooth Frogs off. Protect the windows, protect the tires."

"All while not falling," Sheed said, skeptical.

Otto and Sheed waited for their parents' inevitable argument saying they were kids and they should let the adults handle it.

Solo said, "It's dangerous. But it's more dangerous if we don't trust and rely on each other." He looked to Cinda, "Like we used to. Huh, sis?"

Cinda nodded. "Like we used to. Okay, Alstons. Let's go to work."

"Sweet Easter," Grandma said, slipping the brass knuckles over her fingers, "Who'd have thought a day when we're being chased by carnivorous frogs, bat-people, and a three-headed snake could warm my heart so much. I love you, family."

"We love you, too!"

Sheed boosted Otto to the emergency hatch. He unlatched it, flipped it up and open, then sprang onto the bus roof. Sheed followed. Then Solo and Cinda. Grandma stayed below in case a Tooth Frog or bat-person got past the others; it was the best way to protect the children (and her lower back).

Nyarlathotep's heads sneered at the sight of the Alston

family atop the bus. The monster lunged forward, fueled by hate, getting within a dozen yards of the bus's fender. Otto fired a silver ball bearing from his slingshot, hitting the middle head directly between the eyes. *PLIP.*

"Owwww," the three heads said as one, sounding more offended than hurt.

Otto fired and hit again.

The tanker trucks flanking the boss monster kept shooting Tooth Frogs. Sheed and Cinda swatted some away with their batons, but others stuck and gnawed.

Solo sprayed his cologne on a trio of frogs affixed to his side of the bus. They flailed away into the night, while more tried for the tires. "We have a problem!"

Sheed joined his dad. "Aunt Cinda, I need your baton!"

Solo instinctively knew what his son had planned, as did Cinda. They were all just that good!

As she tossed her baton, Solo threw her his cologne—it was Maneuver #17: weapons swap.

Solo handed the baton to Sheed so the boy held one in each hand. The bus hit a pothole and bucked, bouncing all of the Alstons into the air, but when Sheed and Solo landed, they were on their bellies. Solo grabbed Sheed's legs and swung him over the side of the bus.

Upside down, anchored by his dad, Sheed swatted away the frogs closest to the bus tires. When that side of the bus was clear, Solo yanked Sheed back up top, they slid to the opposite side and repeated the move, ensuring the bus kept rolling.

Meanwhile, Cinda and Otto took down airborne frogs and bat-people with a combination of ball bearings and noxious cologne. Otto glanced over his shoulder at the glowing FISHto's sign — maybe a mile to go. His ammo pouch was low, only a few shots left. "Mom!"

Cinda heard everything she needed to know in the sound of his voice, because that's how moms do, and she said, "Take out the drivers."

Three trucks, and three ball bearings left.

Otto aimed and shot fast. The first ball bearing hit the first tanker's windshield, punching through the glass and off the driver's forehead, knocking the GOO employee unconscious. The truck veered off into a ditch.

Otto sighted the second driver and let fly. Another solid shot. That truck crashed into a roadside billboard.

The last one, though . . .

Ms. Carmichael hit another bump as Otto fired, throwing the shot off. The ball bearing disappeared into the night. His pouch was empty.

Still one truck shooting frogs. Still half a dozen bat-people gaining. Nyarlathotep would catch up eventually. With a half mile to go to FISHto's . . . they weren't going to make it.

"Guys," Otto said.

Below, Grandma shouted, "Some frogs in here!"

Sheed peeked through the hatch and saw gnawed holes in the metal, with Tooth Frogs hopping toward Ms. Carmichael. Grandma and the brave children of D. Franklin Middle intercepted as many as they could and threw them off the bus, but that last tanker kept firing more and more. Soon they'd all be overwhelmed.

Because of me, Sheed thought.

It was him taking the medicine in Warped World to save his life. Him drawing all this new weird to Logan County because of his U-rays. Him . . .

. . . with a brand-new power literally shining bright enough for the whole (weird) world to see.

Sheed's mind exploded, remembering the evening quest. What Otto said when they used their last Key to the City to emerge into the school. "We're the potential?"

We ARE the potential, Sheed thought. *Time to use mine.*

More frogs landed on the bus roof, and Solo leapt ahead of Cinda and Otto, swatting the creatures away. The bat-people were closing in too.

"Rasheed," Solo pleaded.

Sheed came to his father, but not swinging the baton. Instead, he readied his voice. He focused on his belly, trying to imagine a tiny weird light glowing behind his navel. Once the image was in his head, he imagined the light growing larger and glowing brighter. Bright enough to encase his entire body. Strong enough for everything weird to take note.

Otto shouted, "You're doing it, Sheed. You're controlling the glow!"

Glowing Sheed took a breath, and yelled, "STOP! The Weird King commands it!"

The frogs stopped hopping. The bat-people banked away. The last tanker truck swerved and fell behind. Only Nyarlathotep pushed on, angrier than before.

"Stop . . ."

"Right . . ."

"Now!"

Of course the monster would say that. It only ever meant to use Sheed's power for itself.

Nope.

Sheed raised his hand, fingers spread, marveling at his own pulsing yellow glow. *His* U-rays.

The frogs on the bus sat obedient, more like well-trained dogs than hungry amphibians.

Sheed yelled, "Nyarlathotep, spoiler alert! The frogs turn on you. Frogs, attack."

Every Tooth Frog on the bus did a one-eighty-degree turn, flashed their needle teeth in grisly frog smiles, and flung themselves at Nyarlathotep.

"Ack!" the boss monster screamed as a wave of hungry frogs fell upon it. The monster's hide was too tough for the frogs to chew through, but it didn't look exactly comfortable from the pained expression on all three of its faces.

Sheed, Otto, Solo, and Cinda clustered up. Amazed, Solo said, "That glowing thing's a pretty neat trick, son."

Sheed, still speaking in his booming Weird King voice for some reason, said, "It comes in handy."

"Hey!" Ms. Carmichael shouted from below.

Otto ran to the hatch, poked his head in. "What's up?"

"We're about thirty seconds from reaching that fish place."

"Great."

"Eh, not so much," Ms. Carmichael said. "I think those hungry frogs might've chewed the brake line, so I can't really stop the way I want."

"The way you want?" Otto panicked. "Everyone back in the bus."

He leapt down. Sheed and their parents followed. Everyone dived into seats, sensing what was coming.

"Brace yourselves!" Ms. Carmichael said.

She'd let off the gas a while ago, allowing the bus to coast and slow as much as it would, which wouldn't be enough. The bright lobby of Monte FISHto's grew larger, seeming to fill the bus's windshield.

At the last second, Ms. Carmichael turned the wheel, swinging the back side of the bus around so the tail of it collided with the restaurant. The impact rattled everyone to the bones. The screech of metal on metal, the crash of shattered glass, sounded like being at the center of the greatest storm ever.

Then all was still.

Ms. Carmichael leapt from her driver's seat. "Is everyone okay? Anybody hurt?"

Riders sounded off, signaling they were fine. Cinda and Solo checked Otto and Sheed, then Grandma, then themselves. Every passenger on the bus, for the most part, was all right.

How long would they stay that way?
Nyarlathotep was coming!
There was nowhere left to run.
Just as Otto planned.

31

Deal of a Lifetime

OTTO RAN TO MS. CARMICHAEL'S SEAT and flipped the lever that folded the door inward. "Wiki, Leen!"

The school bus butted the counter where four heads popped up from cover. Wiki, Leen, Stu, and Michael Jordan the Goat were covered in dust. Leen shook her head, creating a mini cloud, and said, "That was exciting."

Otto eyed Wiki. "Did you get it done?"

She cocked her thumb at Stu. "Ask him."

Stu grinned wide. "I agree with the proposed terms and have the proper authorization from my main office if you can hold up your end."

Otto twisted so he was staring down the bus aisle. "Mom, I need you! Now!"

Cinda raced to her son. They descended the bus steps together and hopped the counter to join the girls, Stu, and the goat.

A writhing shadow was visible in the distance, closing in on them. Nyarlathotep charging like a serpentine locomotive. Sheed said, "What do you want us to do about that thing?"

"Wait!" Otto said.

Stu produced several typed pages from beneath his batter-spotted apron and placed them on the counter. Cinda skimmed the title page quickly, then looked to her son. "Seriously?"

Otto said, "Yes. Remember the email? Will it work?"

Cinda flipped to the second page, kept skimming. Flipped to the third. "I—I think it might."

Nyarlathotep was nearly there. Solo took the batons from Sheed and placed himself ahead of Grandma, the children, and the bus driver. A final wall of protection. "Cinda!"

"Wait!" Cinda said, flipping to the last page. She told Stu, "Give me a pen."

He already had it waiting.

Cinda snatched it, scribbled her signature in one . . . two . . . three places. Then, "Done."

Nyarlathotep burst through the hole the bus had torn in FISHto's.

"You . . ."

"Sure . . ."

"Are!"

The creature rose to its full height, knocking chunks from the ceiling tiles with its three heads, sneering triumph in its moment of victory.

"Any . . ."

"Last . . ."

"Words?"

"Yes," Cinda said, stepping around the back fender of the bus, with Otto, Stu, and Michael Jordan the Goat in tow. The bundle of papers she'd gotten from Stu were rolled into a tube in her right hand.

Still gloating, Nyarlathotep leaned in close to Cinda, close enough so its breathing ruffled her hair.

Cinda said, "You're demoted!"

Then she popped the middle head with her rolled-up papers. Not enough to hurt, just enough to shame.

"Are . . ."

"You . . ."

"Mad?"

Nyarlathotep lunged as if to strike Cinda but slammed into an invisible wall a few inches shy. The confusion was apparent on all three faces.

"What . . ."

"Is . . ."

"This?"

It lunged again. Hit the wall again.

Cinda clarified. "It's called I'm *your* boss now. And as

long as you're employed by GOO, Inc.—a new subsidiary of the Monte FISHto's Corporation—you take orders from me."

Another lunge, this one of desperate disbelief. Another invisible collision.

"How . . ."

"Did . . ."

"You—"

Otto, perky, said, "Allow me to explain."

Ms. Carmichael gingerly stepped around chunks of debris for a closer listen. "Oh, I gotta hear this."

Sheed, Solo, Grandma, and the D. Franklin Middle kids joined her.

Otto flipped open his Legend Log, checked his notes. "See, while I don't really understand all the corporation and money stuff, I do understand magic, and powers, and how important it is who wields them. Mostly from watching *The Monarch's Gambit*. Which you spoiled for me—I'll never forget that."

"It's all right, baby." Cinda rubbed his shoulder. "We feel your pain."

"Thanks, Mom. As I was saying, you really messed up with that email. Particularly the part that said *we'd like to extend our vast purchasing and deal-making powers to all of you who are still on-site.* See, my mom is *still on-site.*" Otto swept one arm wide, indicating FISHto's, Fry, and the entirety of Logan County—"Do you get it now?"

Ms. Carmichael, wobbly from exhaustion, raised her hand. "I do."

Solo grabbed her raised hand, tugged it down, then walked her to a chair so she could rest. "You might want to sit."

"I might!"

Otto continued. "Nyarlathotep, you should've just fired my mom. It would've almost assured your victory. But, you kept her working for GOO—probably thinking you'd be torturing her later or something—then gave your 'vast purchasing and deal-making powers' to all employees still in Logan County. Including her."

Cinda said, "Since I have your deal-making powers, I made the deal of a lifetime and sold GOO, Inc., to him."

Stu gave a dainty finger wave. "Now you're part of a thriving culinary family that always puts the customer and quality first—"

Otto made a cut-it-out gesture. "Not now, Stu."

"In that deal," said Cinda, "I'm named as the acting chief executive for GOO until I name a replacement and transfer the power to them. Until that time, you belong to me."

The three-headed monster, still defiant, lurched toward Cinda again with no different results than before.

Cinda taunted them. "I think I'm going to transfer you to the Antarctica office."

Nyarlathotep's three heads nodded as if accepting its fate.

"Perhaps you're protected . . ."

"By the deal . . ."

"That you made . . ."

The monster twisted toward Solo and the D. Franklin Middle kids, and spoke with salivating mouths. "But what about them?"

With the bus and counter at their backs, the kids were boxed in, and they cowered. The monster between them and any kind of escape. Nyarlathotep slithered toward them slowly.

Solo, batons ready, said, "Oh no, you—"

The creature's tail snapped like a whip, catching Solo in the side and flinging him clear over the counter, where he crashed into Stu's stove.

"Dad!" Sheed shouted, suddenly more scared than he'd been all night.

Solo pushed himself to his feet, groaning and dazed. Not permanently damaged, but unable to protect the children.

Nyarlathotep loomed over the kids. The jaws of its mouths stretching, its three sets of teeth lengthening and sharpening.

"Since we're in a . . ."

"Restaurant we might as . . ."

"Well have a snack."

Ms. Carmichael, re-energized by the children left in her care being in such grave danger, flung herself on Nyarlathotep's tail, "Leave them kids alone!"

Cinda followed her lead. As did Stu, Grandma, Otto, Sheed, Wiki, and Leen.

Even Windy, who'd been hovering outside the building per Wiki and Leen's instruction, zoomed in and blew a mighty gale to counter the creature's momentum.

All attempted to halt the monster's efforts to eat the D. Franklin Middle kids, with little success. Nyarlathotep was an ancient, powerful, and evil creature, reveling in its very last chance to hurt Logan County and the city of Fry by striking at its children. Its potential.

Every Legendary and Epic hero in the room, along with their allies, strained against the monster's slippery muscle. The good guys were giving it everything they had.

"Sheed!" screamed Otto, his fingers aching from gripping Nyarlathotep's scales.

"Otto!" Sheed yelled back, stabbing two Afro picks into the ridges of hard reptilian flesh.

Neither had a maneuver for this, and their sneakers lost traction as they were dragged along.

Then . . . they weren't.

Nyarlathotep wasn't moving toward its meal of sixth graders anymore. Instead it reared up, seeing what they all saw, likely as puzzled as they all were.

"What . . ."

"Is . . ."

"This?"

"The goat," Sheed said, hushed.

Michael Jordan the Goat had positioned himself between the monster and the children.

Wiki hopped off Nyarlathotep's tail, as did everyone else who'd been hanging on for dear life.

"Aren't . . ."

"You . . ."

"Cute."

Michael Jordan the Goat scratched at the dusty floor with one of his forelegs, the way a bull might before charging.

What happened next would be one of those "Remember That Time" memories everyone bearing witness would have for the rest of their lives. The kind of thing that would come up anytime they got together, whether they'd traveled to the corners of the earth and back, or grown up to live different lives in different cities. Whether their adventures became wholly separate things beyond Fry and Logan County—the Alstons doing their thing, while the Ellisons did theirs. Whether five, ten, or fifty years passed during which some of them—Grandma, Solo, Cinda, Ms. Carmichael—became loving and cherished memories themselves. The kind of memory that helped you recall all the things that made you friends and family.

None of them would ever forget what Michael Jordan the Goat did at crunch time!

The goat rushed forward, leapt with grace of a ballet dancer, and jabbed his horns into the monster's middle chin.

Nyarlathotep's head snapped back, its three mouths stretching into a prolonged "Owwww!"

A shock wave spread from the point of impact in a Saturn-like ring that flung various bits of dust and debris backwards as Nyarlathotep left the ground completely. That same shock wave knocked everyone standing onto

their butts. Even Windy was whooshed to the back of the restaurant.

Nyarlathotep kept rising, with a speed and force that closely resembled a rocket at liftoff. Michael Jordan the Goat's headbutt sent the creature through the FISHto's roof, into the night sky, end over end, its pained screams fading with distance that stretched and stretched as the beast grew smaller and smaller, becoming a dark pinprick on the backdrop of the moon.

The goat, who seemed to hang in the air for several seconds, finally landed, giving them a wink and what Otto interpreted as a goat shrug.

The D. Franklin Middle School kids erupted with applause.

"Is it over?" Otto said, having a hard time accepting what seemed to be true. "Did we save Logan?

Cinda stroked her son's cheek. "I think we did."

Solo climbed debris to get to Sheed, massaging his sore ribs as he did. At his son's side, he reached for the boy's shoulder warily, stopping an inch shy, waiting for permission. Sheed nodded, granting it. Solo scooped him up in a long overdue embrace.

Grandma joined her family, looking everyone up and down. "For our next outing, I think we should just go to a buffet."

Stu said, "Why a buffet when you can have a Cra-Burger, Filet Fries, and a whale-sized drink?"

Michael Jordan the Goat *ba-aaaed*.

Sheed said, "I'mma be real with you. You may have helped us save Logan County, but most of the food here still nasty."

No one disagreed. Not even Stu.

32

If Petey Thunkle Can Do It

THE NEXT FEW SUNRISES saw Logan County and the town of Fry slowly shifting back to normal—or as normal as the cozily strange place could ever be.

Under Cinda's leadership in her new role as the chief executive in charge of GOO: A Monte FISHto's Company (wow, business stuff was the true weirdness, if you asked the Legendary Alston Boys), she made some swift changes to improve the company's relationship with the county folk.

In the moments immediately after Michael Jordan the Goat butted Nyarlathotep into the stratosphere, Cinda ordered all the GOO employees who'd turned into gigantic bat-people to put their wings away and inform the Money Zombies they could return to the homes they'd sold. There was resistance from the Money Zombies in the form of moans and pointing at the checks each of them clutched so tightly.

Cinda seemed to understand these strange gestures even if they were nonsensical to the children. She consulted quietly with Stu, then climbed atop the counter to address the hordes herself. "The homes still belong to you, but you can also keep the money. Consider it an apology for the damage done to you. An investment in the community."

The Money Zombies moan-cheered and shuffled off with wide smiles.

Except for Mr. Rickard.

He tried to shuffle on home, but the boys stopped him.

"Sir," Otto said.

Mr. Rickard grunted, his pupils already shifting from the zombified dollar signs to regular eyes, Nyarlathotep's spell slowly fading.

Sheed said, "There's something you should know."

They broke the bad news. Sheed did the talking, while Otto sort of mimed Mr. Rickard's house exploding. By the time they finished, he seemed completely free of the corrupting influence that had taken hold of him. That was the best the boys could figure. After all, they didn't think a full-fledged Money Zombie would faint the way he did.

#

The next day, Cinda ordered the company to rebuild Mr. Rickard's house with improvements that ensured it would be extra normal, as he requested. He was grateful.

#

While most of the townspeople adjusted to the FISH-to's-GOO merger relatively well, Fry itself was not without scars. Buildings and businesses bought during Nyarlathotep's reign only returned to their original state if the sticky, nasty snot hadn't taken complete hold of the parts below the surface, what you couldn't see.

Nice Dream Ice Cream shop did not come back. The original owner moved on, and Riches Brew remained.

"Is there something we can do?" Sheed asked Solo. They'd descended beneath the town together, Sheed agreeing to spend more time with his dad because if their parents' plans remained the same and they'd all be leaving Logan County soon, he might as well get used to it.

In the catacombs beneath Fry, with powerful flashlights sweeping over the cables and supports of the coffee shop, the thick—there's no other way to say it, *goo*—remained.

Solo said, "Sometime things can't go back the way they were. Doesn't mean we can't make the best of a new thing."

"I still don't want Black Bean Lemon Drop gelato," Sheed said.

"I know. There might be other good flavors, though. If you're willing to try."

Solo's voice was quiet, and he kept finding other stuff to look at that wasn't his son. Sheed thought about what his dad just said, and how he seemed kind of embarrassed that he'd said it. The Otto Voice in his head—a constant thing he'd never tell Otto about because then he'd know Sheed missed him when they weren't together—said, *I don't think he's talking about gelato.*

To use a bit of deductive skill (Otto would be proud), the new thing Sheed's dad was really speaking on was whatever came next for the two of them. If Sheed was willing to try too.

"I'm down for new stuff. If you're down to stick around when things get hard."

Solo nodded. "I will. I promise you that."

As Grandma would say, *That's the best any of us can do.*

#

While Sheed spent a bunch of time with his dad and Cinda spent a bunch of time down at City Hall with Mayor Ahmed trying to get as much of Fry fixed as possible, Otto ran down the to-do list he'd made, checking off tasks he felt were Super Important. In other times they would've been Regular Important, but they got the Super tag because . . . because . . .

He might not get the chance to do them later.

As far as he knew, Mom's and Uncle Solo's plans hadn't

changed. The Legendary Alstons would not be a part of Fry's next big adventure, or Logan County's ongoing history. He needed to make sure the place he'd known as home most of his life got left in good shape.

OTTO'S SUPER IMPORTANT TO-DO LIST, CONT'D

6. ~~Negotiate a peace treaty with the Locker Gnomes~~ (I showed them where the teachers keep their supplies, and the little guys went wild; they seemed to really appreciate the come up.)

7. ~~Find Mr. Feltspur~~ (Him and his kite were stuck in a tree at the county outskirts, but he was okay.)

8. ~~Confirm Dr. Medina is back in business and her animals came home because for most of them she really was home~~ (Confirmed! The animals are back and getting strong!)

9. ~~Find Bernard the monkey~~ (IN THE TREE NEXT TO MR. FELTSPUR'S

TREE!! WHY DIDN'T I JUST LOOK
UP AND TO THE LEFT?)

10. Go see Wiki.

It was the last thing on his list. He tried to think of
other important things, but nothing came up. Biking over
to the Ellison farm, his deductive mind couldn't stop analyzing that last to-do item.

Go see Wiki.

Not Wiki *and* Leen because, honestly, he didn't want to
see the *Epic Ellisons, plural.* He wanted to see *an Epic Ellison.* Badly. That was new.

He turned onto the long dirt road that cut through
the Ellison cornfields, a light breeze whispering between
the stalks and pushing him along. When the road yawned
wide, revealing the big red house, he thought about going
up to the porch and ringing the bell, but because of what
happened with Leen's robotic decoys and the countermeasures, the girls were grounded.

Still, Otto had to see her.

He dropped his bike under their bedroom window,
scooped up a handful of pebbles, then tossed them one
by one, tapping their windowpane. On the fourth pebble,
a face appeared in the window. Wiki and Leen's uncle
Percy.

He yanked the window up as Otto tossed a fifth pebble. "Boy!"

The rock popped Percy Ellison in the forehead, then rebounded off into the corn.

"Ouch," Percy said, rubbing an already swelling welt. "I'm going to—"

Percy disappeared into the shadows of the house and emerged on the front porch a few seconds later, with his round belly hanging over his belt. He twisted in Otto's direction and stomped toward the boy with his fists clenched.

Otto supposed he could've—should've?—run. When the instinct arose, it was immediately countered by a new voice in his head. It was that of TimeStar, the traveler from the future who claimed to be an older version of Otto himself on the last day of summer. One of the final things uttered before he disappeared through his portal home. *"Wiki Ellison . . . ain't so bad."*

Otto, though terrified, stood his ground, prepared to take whatever punishment Percy planned to deliver. A second from Percy snatching Otto by the collar, there was a *WHOOSH* sound, followed by Percy yelling, "Hey!"

He levitated off the ground in a bubble of green energy. The beam projecting the energy tracked back to a ray gun in the hands of Leen Ellison. "Yes!" she said. "Petey Thunkle isn't the only one who can crack antigravity."

Percy pounded the inside of the bubble with the meaty part of his fist. "Girl! Let me out this thing!"

Leen angled her ray gun in the opposite direction, and Percy swung far away from Otto, as if he was the wrecking ball at the end of an invisible chain. "Hey, hey, hey!"

"I'm just going to take you for a little walk, Unk." Leen directed her attention to Wiki, who appeared on the porch steps, arms crossed. "Maybe you can keep Otto company while I run a few more tests, Wik."

They had one of the moments Otto knew well from when he and Sheed did it. Communicating volumes with a look. His stomach fluttered.

Leen walked into the corn, dragging an increasingly angry Percy along until the stalks swallowed them both, leaving Otto and Wiki alone. Wiki came off the steps, arms still crossed, her lips pinched into a flat line. "Your face is weird."

"Weird how?"

"I'm unsure. It's a new tic. I haven't seen it enough to be able to identify it with one hundred percent certainty."

"So guess."

"That's what amateurs do. You and Sheed guess a lot, huh?"

"Ha ha!"

She stiffened. "You did your sarcasm thing, then your face slipped back to the other tic. You're—you're sad."

Otto didn't deny it.

"Why are you sad, Otto?"

He'd dropped the pebbles he'd been tossing at the

window, nudged some with his sneaker. "I think we're leaving soon."

"Oh. That's — oh."

He looked her in the eye; her face was sad as well.

"How soon?" she asked.

He shrugged. "No one's said anything. But they're being so quiet about it, I'm expecting them to spring it on us any day now. I wanted to, I don't know, I wanted—"

Wiki closed the gap between them quickly so hardly no space remained. She said, "If it's okay with you, I'm going to kiss you on the cheek. Is that all right?"

"It is."

She pecked him on the cheek, then backed up a step.

The place her lips touched him burned with the most pleasant fire Otto had ever known. He started to say something, but there were no words.

Wiki said, "With current technology we can keep in touch in a number of different ways. Is it too much to presume you may visit Logan County from time to time? To see your grandma?"

"I think she's coming, too. And Sheed's going somewhere else. And it's all a big mess, Wiki. So, I don't know."

"Well, my brains, Leen's tech, there's really nothing anchoring *us* here. Maybe it's time for the Epic Ellisons to branch out, too."

Maybe. "In case you don't, though, I wanted to tell you—shoot, you kissing me on the cheek sorta knocked all of this out of order. I was going to say it's been fun battling you, and even if we don't see each other for a while, we'll definitely cross paths again, and when we do, you can bet—dang it, Wiki!"

"What? Why are you stopping your monologue?"

"Because I think I want another kiss. If that's okay."

"I give you permission."

He stepped forward and kissed *her* cheek. Wiki, then, did something he'd only ever seen her do once before. Blush.

Her ponytail began to sway in a soft breeze, like something from the lovey-dovey movies Grandma liked. Otto looked over his shoulder at the elemental. "That's real cute, Windy."

The disembodied head grinned and flew away.

Then Leen exploded out of the corn, her ray gun smoking. "Antigravity has a short battery life!"

Percy came on the run, also smoking, his hair standing on end, singed.

Wiki ran then, too. Side by side with her sister, looking over her shoulder at Otto. "We'll see each other again, Octavius Alston."

The girls disappeared into the corn. Followed by their angry uncle.

Otto had no doubt.

Even though he just saw Wiki, she'd JUST run away from him — he missed her already.

That . . . was new, too.

33

Time for a Change

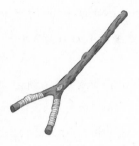

ON SATURDAY, EVEN THOUGH A MONSTER had spoiled the twist and they all knew Don Glö's long-kept secret, Otto, Sheed, and Grandma finally sat down to watch *The Monarch's Gambit* together.

Perhaps for the last time.

Cinda was at yet another City Hall meeting. Solo was seeing Bernard off (he'd gotten a tip on where his missing paw might be). It was nice to know they were near and just as nice to feel something like the olden days. With one difference.

Instead of their usual positions—Sheed on the carpet, Otto on the couch, and Grandma in the old recliner that belonged to their grandpa—they squeezed onto the couch together. Three Legendary Alstons, all in a row.

They made it through the episode without an

interruption, amazed. Hearing about a thing wasn't the same as seeing it yourself, or feeling it. Well worth the wait.

"That was awesome," Sheed said over the closing credits.

As soon as the theme music faded, the sound of a heavy engine chuffed in the distance and grew closer. Louder.

The three of them ran to the window. It was a moving van.

Followed by Cinda's big ole rental and Solo in Grandma's car.

Otto faced Sheed, who blinked rapidly because his eyes burned. Today was the day, then.

They gathered in the foyer, as scared as when Tooth Frogs were chewing their way inside. The door swung inward, and despite the circumstances, Otto couldn't fight the rush of pure joy that flooded him.

"Dad!" He hurled himself at his father.

"Hey, champ!" DeMarcus swung his son in a circle, spinning away from the door, clearing a path for Cinda and Solo.

The siblings hovered. Cinda taken by the sight of her two guys loving on each other and Solo giving Sheed the affectionate what-up nod followed by a fist bump that was their thing now.

Then the reality set in. Otto stiffened in his dad's arms, and DeMarcus placed him back on the floor. Sheed focused on some random section of wallpaper. This was awkward.

Cinda said, "Hey, what's with those long faces?"

Otto said, "Dad's here to help us move. You're taking us away from Logan." Otto chanced a glance at Sheed. "You're splitting us up now."

Cinda's head bobbed, as if she needed time to process that jarring bit of reality. She said, "I think we should talk about Mr. Archie."

Otto couldn't believe this. Another *analogy?* Why couldn't grownups just say what they mean? For once! He felt very close to a full-on Sheed-style tantrum. As angry as he was, he still knew better than to pop off in front of his mom. He was mad, not reckless.

So, fine. Analogy time.

Cinda said, "Mr. Archie's leaving town."

"We *beat* Nyarlathotep!" said Sheed, shocked. "There shouldn't be any more checks to brainwash him."

"He's not brainwashed. He could've stayed, continuing to run his business as he always has. He doesn't want to, though. Not since he found out he's going to be a grandpa."

The boys were slightly stunned. Mr. Archie . . . a grandpa? That meant his daughter, Anna, and her husband, trillionaire Petey Thunkle, were going to have a baby! That kid was going to be born the richest kid in the world! That was kind of amazing. But . . .

"What's going to happen to his store, and his house?" Otto asked. Also, what kind of analogy was this? What did it have to do with splitting him, Sheed, and Grandma up?

Cinda rooted in her purse. "I don't know about his store.

I'm sure he has a plan in place. As for his house, well." She produced a couple of keys on a simple key ring. "I guess that's up to us — though your bedroom will be one hundred percent your responsibility."

Otto . . . couldn't think. His head whipped to his dad.

DeMarcus said, "What can I say, son? Mr. Archie isn't the only one who wants to be closer to his family."

Otto slowly regained the ability to speak and deduce. "This isn't an analogy. You actually bought Mr. Archie's house."

Then he scooted around his mom to the doorway, pointing at the moving truck and recognizing an obvious clue he'd missed. The big boxy vehicle sat heavy on its tires, straining the suspension. It wasn't an empty truck to be filled with things they were taking away, it was packed with his mom and dad's belongings. "That's stuff you're moving in. We're staying in Logan County!"

Cinda nodded. "Beautiful deduction, son."

Otto, his mom, and his dad collided in a big group hug. Overjoyed times three. But, when Otto peered over his mom's shoulder at Sheed, he felt new fear. *He* was staying in Logan County. Was his cousin going to be able to say the same?

The foyer got quiet. Sheed waited for bad news. Grandma stared at Solo the way she probably stared at him when he was a five-year-old and needed to explain how crayon got on her walls.

Solo, seemingly in his own world, became alert. "Oh, right. Us? Sheed, we're staying, too."

Cinda said, "Really, bro? Just like that?"

"I'm not one for all that drama, sis. Sheed, I got a job."

Sheed, cautiously happy, but a little afraid to ask, said, "Huh?"

For a nightmarish moment, Sheed had a vision of his dad behind the counter at Riches Brew serving up some especially nasty gelato, like Toothpaste and Orange Juice flavored.

Solo—maybe liking a little bit of drama—swept the folds of his long leather duster aside, revealing a golden star on his belt. Engraved across the width of it, a single word: *Sheriff.*

"Dad, you're the Sheriff of Fry now?"

"That's part of the deal, son."

Grandma, skeptical but grinning, said, "*You're* the po-po? Didn't see that coming."

Solo said, "After the former sheriff took his GOO money and skipped town, the mayor needed someone with weird experience who also wasn't consistently terrified."

Otto said, "*Part* of the deal!" To his mom, "What's the rest of the deal?"

"Well," said Cinda, "since I still have Nyarlathotep's

deal-making powers, and given the massive stake GOO: A FISHto's Company has in the town, Mayor Ahmed was highly motivated to maintain the community feel of it all. He was open for some bargaining. I was tired of trying to make evil sound good for the sake of my job, so we found a mutually beneficial agreement to do some actual good."

Grandma said, "Now, I gots to hear this."

"I think you'll like this, Ma," said Cinda. "In exchange for a permanent leadership position in Fry's Community Development Office and a few other perks, I signed over my control in the FISHto's-GOO arrangement to the town. Meaning . . . neither of those companies will be able to change Fry, without Fry's permission, EVER! AGAIN!"

Otto and Sheed hooted. Hollered. Danced like there were ants in their pants.

Otto said, "Dad, what about you?"

DeMarcus said, "I'm done with GOO, too! With all this business opportunity popping up in Fry, they need more number crunchers down at City Hall. One of the perks of your mom's deal was getting me a position here in town."

Grandma jumped into the conversation. "Sounds like y'all did a fine job with all that wheeling and dealing, so where's that leave me? You two good at making big decisions without consulting who you deciding for."

Cinda and Solo looked incredibly hurt.

Grandma had a point, though. Where did all this leave her, and her house?

Sheed said, "Dad, are me, you, and Grandma staying here?"

"*I'm* not staying here," Solo said, adamant. "Sorry, Ma. My bedtime and curfew days are long behind me."

"That's why you got them bags under your eyes," Grandma mumbled.

"Son, there's this real nice guy at City Hall named Wallace who wouldn't shut up about the condos in town. So I got one. Plenty of room for both of us."

Sheed's heart sank. "You're still splitting me, Otto, and Grandma up?"

Otto, no longer worried about popping off, because sometimes you had to pop off, said, "Have you forgotten about Grandma's sugar and blood pressure? We help her with her medicine. Did you negotiate how we're going to keep doing that from Mr. Archie's house and the condo? Do you have any more perks?"

Without realizing it, the boys had settled into one of their defensive maneuvers, flanking Grandma as they had on the night of the Tooth Frog storm. Both expected some typically infuriating parental response. Something like "This Is Grown Folks' Business" or "You'll Understand When You're Older."

Instead, DeMarcus whistled. "Well dag-gone, Cinda and Solo, they are really reading y'all right now!"

Cinda and Solo laughed, unable to deny it.

"What's so funny?" Sheed just about growled, and his U-ray glow pulsed.

Solo's laughter dried up. "Whoa, son, settle down. Let us finish."

Cinda said, "This is the best perk of all. I worked it out where Ma can stay here in her house, and if you want, you can stay here, too. Sure, there's a room for you at our place, Otto."

"And a room for you at my condo, Sheed," said Solo.

"But," Cinda said, "you only have to use them when you want to. It's your choice. You've earned it."

Solo said, "We'd be fools to break up such a legendary team . . . even if we all were in the same county."

The wave of relief that hit Otto almost knocked him down. Sheed stopped glowing. Grandma nodded, said, "I raised a pretty good bunch here."

Solo said, "You did, Ma."

Cinda snapped her fingers. "Oh, one more thing."

The boys got nervous again when she dipped outside and returned a moment later with an orange bag featuring the PeteyTech logo. "Final part of the deal. I told the mayor that if we're going to have legendarily epic teams handling the stranger occurrences around town, they needed some modern tech."

Grandma saw where this was going and sucked her teeth. "I take back what I said about raising a good bunch."

Solo said, "Ma!"

The boys weren't listening. Cinda fished the two brick-sized boxes from the bag and presented them. Otto and Sheed were just about vibrating with excitement over their new, sleek, top-of-the-line ThunklePhones!

Otto turned the orange box over in his hands, admiring the beautifully simple design. Sheed already had the plastic torn away and was prying the box top off with his finger-nails. Both boys ran upstairs, the worries of the day lost in the joy of new toys.

"Thanks, Mom!"

"Thanks, Aunt Cinda!"

Solo said, "No one wanna thank me for being a part of the fun? Cool, cool. I see how it is."

Otto's Cloud-Based Legendary Log 1.0

Entry #1

ThunklePhones are so sweet! The smartest smartphones on earth. "So smart . . . they're dangerous!" according to the original, discontinued ad campaign. Anyway . . .

Turns out the mayor sent a couple of phones to the Ellisons, too. Sheed was doing a lot of texting with Leen until she decided to take hers apart and modify it. So he went downstairs to shoot hoops on the dirt patch out back with his dad. They're playing HORSE, and Uncle Solo already has an R.

I might go down with them, Otto thought. *Soon.* Wiki's phone was still functional though . . .

Deduction: There will be time to go play later. All the time in the world. Nobody in our family is going anywhere.

ThunkleMessenger

Otto: Hey Wiki!

Wiki: Hey Otto!

Otto: Can I ask you a question?

Wiki: You just did, but you may ask another.

Otto: Wanna ride into town and try some of that new gelato stuff? I heard it might be interesting . . .

ACKNOWLEDGMENTS

These are getting so much harder to write.

There are always so many people to thank when a book makes it into the world, and I become increasingly terrified that I'm missing someone. There are the members of the Versify family (Kwame Alexander, Margaret Raymo, Dapo Adeola, Derick Brooks, Whitney Leader-Picone, Tara Shanahan, Amanda Acevedo, Ciera Burch, etc.). The members of my actual family (Adrienne, Mom, the siblings, the nieces and nephews). The publishing family (Jamie, Carmen, Eric [Reid], Jennifer). The extended publishing family (Meg, Gbemi, Dhonielle, Sona, Tiffany, Nic, Jason, Eric [Smith], Jeff, Ellen, Preeti, Lilliam, etc.).

And never let me forget you, Dear Reader.

Thank you for coming back to Logan County time and time again. Otto, Sheed, Wiki, Leen, and me will be here for as long as you want and/or need us, and I thank you for the privilege of telling you these stories.